MERCY
&
Truth

DR. PAUL A. KINGSBURY

—

Discovering God's Perfect Blend for Balance

DR. PAUL A. KINGSBURY

REFORMERS UNANIMOUS INTERNATIONAL

PO Box 15732, Rockford, IL 61132
Visit our website at www.reformu.com.
Printed in Canada
Cover design by Benjamin Smith and Jeremy N. Jones
Cover photo by Jeremy N. Jones

Dr. Paul A. Kingsbury, 1953-
Mercy & Truth: Discovering God's Perfect Blend for Balance
Dr. Paul A. Kingsbury

ISBN 978-1-61623-565-9

{Contents

{Mercy and Truth Dedication

It is with sincere gratitude and heartfelt devotion that I dedicate this book on God's mercy and truth to my dear mother-in-law, Irene Clapp. Her life was a consistent demonstration of these divine attributes that have captured my attention and punctuated my preaching for the past several months. Mom Clapps' departure to heaven in 2008 was mourned by all who were privileged to know this incredible woman, including her only son-in-law.

My observations of Dianne's mother were not from a distance. As a resident of our community and a faithful member of our church, I witnessed firsthand as she poured her life into serving the Lord and our family during the final decade of her earthly journey. Mom did not come into my life only in her latter years. No, I knew her as a "second mom" throughout my childhood days in southwestern Michigan. Mrs. Clapp taught me the Bible in children's church at Bethel Baptist in downtown Kalamazoo. My earliest recollections of this remarkable lady place her with the Word of God in her hand exuberantly explaining the finer points of an exciting event out of biblical history. The Clapp home became a second home to me through a "best friend" relationship with her son, David; and subsequently, a love that led to a friendship and marriage with their daughter, Dianne. Summer Saturdays at their lake house in my teen years honed my love and respect for this woman of such compassion and commitment.

When Dianne's father passed away in January of 1977, we were honored to see the stabilizing impact of mom's favoured relationship with God. She embraced His mercy and truth through the sorrows of widowhood and then the sickness and death of her only son. She consistently sought to live like the Lord that she loved. She succeeded.

Even as pancreatic cancer took over her body and wreaked its devastating mission, Mom Clapp never succumbed to self-pity or depression. Her commitment to living her life mercifully and truthfully was never compromised in those difficult days. Pointed yet positive; opinionated, yet rarely offensive; mom was always quick to praise and slow to criticize.

If there is a library in heaven for the writings of sincere, yet admittedly fallible, Christian authors; or if the dear Lord allows our loved ones there to glimpse down at the goings on in the lives of those they loved here, I hope that Mom Clapp will smile and derive joy from knowing that her mercy and truth is still impacting the lives of all who are helped by this treatise.

Dr. Paul Kingsbury

Pastor Paul Kingsbury
September 2009

Mercy & Truth

n the latter months of 1971, I became a coffee drinker. Being away from home for the first time at eighteen years of age and for the first time partaking of this "adult" drink was a rite of passage of sorts for this freshman Bible college student. Dad and mom refused my requests for a taste of their Maxwell House concoction on the grounds of "stunting my growth." This I found to be somewhat ludicrous when considering the apparent absence of size inhibiting forces derived from the daily doses they imbibed. Anyway, my first cup of the black brew was so significant that I can remember the exact location and specific circumstances of my initial encounter.

I had been invited to serve the Lord on week-ends in the church that I now pastor, North Love Baptist Church in Rockford, Illinois. The preacher, Dr. James Alley, assigned a young Christian couple, Jerry and Hope Bredeson, to be my home away from home parents. The lower level of their spacious ranch style house had a guest room, and I became their Saturday through Sunday son. My first visit to their Maple Avenue residence became my initiation into the brotherhood of "java junkies."

With introductions out of the way and my duffel bag secured in my basement bedroom, I was handed an oversized ceramic mug by "Mrs. B" with the instruction to "hold it out here, and I'll fill it up." As the queen of the home poured a generous amount of piping hot joe into the cup, she inquired of my previous coffee drinking experience. I had none of course. This discovery then led to a rapidly enunciated piece of news that it would be impossible for me to live in the Bredeson home except I become a participant in swallowing copious amounts of her "Baptist brew," as she called it. I was happy to oblige.

Happy, that is, until my first taste. Having already acknowledged that I was a coffee virgin, it seemed as if everyone in the kitchen that significant night stared in silent anticipation of my response to this new taste. What a surprise! My nose was telling me that this percolated beverage was going to produce a virtual wow for my taste buds. But, my smeller lied. Not only did this stuff not taste good, but it tasted bad! Out of my memory banks an analogy of coffee tasting like battery acid emerged. Although I had never tasted the liquid inside of a twelve volt electrical container, I was certain that the anti-coffee drinkers were right.

My new "parents" recognized that an adverse reaction was coming; and so, before I could say anything, I was given a verbal rescue. "Don't worry. Most people don't like the taste of coffee the first time," I was informed. "It's an acquired taste," someone posed. I have to admit that their voices of hope for this eighteen-year-old recruit did little to lessen the acrid taste lingering in my offended mouth. Swallowing the coffee was difficult. Swallowing their advice? Impossible.

Just about then, a miracle occurred. Oh, I am not speaking of the walk on water, divine intervention type of supernatural events spoken of in the Bible. However, the One who turned water into wine also created two very important additives for coffee, which, when blended together with that which was in the cup I held in my hand, created one of nature's best tastes. Cream and sugar came to my rescue.

This brings me to the purpose for writing a book on mercy and truth. Mercy and truth are two attributes of both God and godly, balanced, mature people. In the nearly two dozen times these companions are mentioned side by side in the Scriptures, we see their tremendous power to transform relationships and provide direction and reason for life's experiences. Proverbs 3 verse 4 refers to these benefits of mercy and truth as favour and good understanding. And, these blessings are available for both our vertical relationship with God and horizontal relationships with people!

Achieving the perfect blend of mercy and truth, then, has been my personal goal in studying these topics in Scripture as well as my pastoral aim in behalf of the wonderful folk who call me their pastor and preacher at North Love Baptist Church. Unfortunately, much suffering and frustration occurs in people's lives when we fail to become individuals of both mercy and truth. Blending both together in appropriate amounts and distributing them to others faithfully minimizes problems and maximizes potential. God has the perfect blend of mercy and truth, and His testimony will become our guide in this eighteen chapter study.

I pray that God will show you, the reader, His personal goals for you in this matter of blending mercy and truth as you read, study, and meditate upon this subject.

chapter 1

Eliezer's Astute Observation

"And the man (Eliezer, the servant of Abraham) *bowed his head and worshipped the Lord. And he said blessed be the Lord God of my master Abraham, who hath not left destitute my master of his mercy and his truth. I, being in the way, the Lord led me to the house of my master's brethren."* —*Genesis 24:26&27*

In Bible days, names carried a great weight of meaning, and people chose names for their children based on the hopes that they had for their lives. For example, after waiting for twenty-five years for his birth, Abraham and Sarah named their son Isaac, which means laughter. Abraham's house was run by his chief steward, a man named Eliezer, which means God is my help. Abraham trusted him implicitly, assigning him the task of seeking a bride for Isaac.

When Eliezer undertook this task, he did not know exactly how to fulfill it, but he did know where to turn for help. He prayed for God's guidance and found Rebekah willing to water his camels—the sign which he had asked God to provide. As he recounted his journey to Rebekah and her family, he made a very astute observation about the nature and character of God. He said that God is both mercy and truth.

God is mercy; He is filled with kindness. If you get to know God like Eliezer knew Him, you will find that God refrains from bringing upon our lives painful, but deserved consequences. I am so grateful we do not get what we deserve! God is ever merciful. In fact, His mercies are new every morning and great is his faithfulness. (Lamentations 3:22) His mercy is, as the Bible declares, from everlasting unto everlasting and endures forever (Psalm 100:5, Psalm 136:25).

God is also truth; He is always right and always righteous. He never makes an error. He never makes a mistake. And He sees and knows everything. The God of the Bible is brutally honest with His people. He does not overlook our transgressions. He chastens every true child of His. (Hebrews 12: 6) Jesus said, "I am the way, the truth, and the life." (John 14:6)

Understanding this balanced nature of God—full of both mercy and truth—helps us understand who He is; it also helps us understand how He expects us to live. He is both completely merciful and completely truthful. Let's look at a few of the places in Scripture where we see these two traits together.

Genesis 32:10 says, *"I am not worthy* (Jacob is praying to God) *of the least of all the mercy and of all the truth."*

Exodus 34:6 says, *"and the Lord passed by before him* (Moses) *and proclaimed the Lord, the Lord God is merciful and gracious, long-suffering and abundant in goodness and truth."*

Psalm 25:10 says, *"all the paths of the Lord are mercy and truth."*

Psalm 40:10&11 says, *"I have not hid thy righteousness within my heart. I have declared thy faithfulness and thy salvation. I have not concealed thy loving kindness* (the same word often translated "mercy") *and thy truth."*

Psalm 57:3 says, *"He shall ascend from heaven and save me from the reproach of him that would swallow me up. Selah* (that means stop and think about this) *God shall send forth his mercy and his truth."*

Psalm 57:10 says, *"For thy mercy is great unto the heavens and thy truth unto the clouds."*

Psalm 61:7 says, *"He shall abide before God forever O prepare mercy and truth which may preserve him."*

Psalm 69:13 says, *"But as for me my prayer is unto thee O Lord, in an acceptable time O God. In the multitude of thy mercy hear me in the truth of thy salvation."*

This theme of the balance between God's mercy and truth appears again and again in His Word. Why? Because God knows we need to learn this principle. God knows we need to know this about His nature and character. God knows we need to develop the balance between these two traits in our lives.

It is absolutely imperative that you get to know who God is and what He is like. There was a time in my life when I was basically interested in what God could do for me. I read the Bible; I studied it from the point of view of what God could do for me, to make my life easier, to make it more successful. As I grew in grace and in my relationship with the Lord, I became more impressed with my responsibility to serve and live for Him. I haven't lost that appreciation of what He does for me, but that has been replaced and I am motivated with a greater burden of what I can do for him. The more I understand about Him, the better I know Him, the longer I serve Him, the more I want to honor and please Him with every day of my life.

As we have seen, the observation that Eliezer made about God's balanced nature is often repeated in Scripture, but his declaration is the first time we find these two characteristics of God joined together. That brings us to this question: how did Eliezer reach this understanding? By studying how Eliezer learned of God's mercy and truth, we can learn this vital principle for our own lives.

The key to Eliezer's understanding is found in Genesis 24:27 where he says "I being in the way." When Eliezer talks of "being in the way," he is speaking about much more than just his journey to find a bride for Isaac; he is speaking of a lifetime journey of faith and walking with God. Eliezer had followed Abraham and faithfully served him for many years. During that time, he had seen God work in miraculous ways, protecting and providing for their needs. He had seen a man of great faith pray and receive answers to his prayers. He had learned by experience that God was both mercy and truth. Eliezer's faith was a well-worn path for his feet to follow, even when he went to places he had never been before.

Many Christians who fail do so because they have never personally discovered God's character for themselves. They don't grasp how merciful and how truthful God is because they go in and out of the way. It is not a well-worn path with them. There is something that comes with staying in the way that brings you to a greater appreciation and recognition of the greatness and goodness of God. The more you walk with Him, the more you talk with Him, the more you serve Him with your life; the more your way becomes plain and clear.

We live in a fast-food culture. We don't want to wait for anything. And sometimes I think we want a "fast food God." We say, "All I want is a dynamic relationship with God." My friend, make it your life's purpose then. It is not something that you go and pay $2.29 for at a drive-through window. We do not get God that way. You've got to get in the way, and you've got to stay in the way. When everybody else is going out of the way, you stay in the way.

My wife and I have been married for 35 years. Sometimes people ask me, "How can I have a best friend relationship with my spouse such as you and Mrs. Kingsbury have?" You stay in the way. You stay courting each other; you stay loving each other; you stay right with each other; and you stay spending time with each other. My wife and I knew each other all of our lives before we got married. If you asked me on my wedding day if I knew Dianne, I would have said, "Yes." But, what I knew about her then pales in comparison to how well I know her now. We have spent these years "in the way"; and as a result, we have a close and sweet relationship.

I have watched people who get in and out of the way. One day they're on; the next day they're off. One day they're in; the next day they're out. They wonder why they don't know God very well. They come and ask me why their walk with God is not personal and intimate. You will never get to know God unless you get in the way and stay there. It is so easy to get out of the way. The root meaning of one of the words for sin is "to go off the path or out of the way." "Prone to wander Lord I feel it, prone to leave the God the God I love."

Eliezer was in the way for a long time. We first meet him in Genesis 15 when God first promised Abraham a son. That was more than fifty years before the events of Genesis 24 when Eliezer talked about being in the way! Five decades of faith, five decades of humble service, five decades of answered prayers, and five decades of doing the will of God prepared Eliezer to trust His mercy and truth when he needed help and direction for his life. God gave a revelation of His character to Eliezer—that He was filled with mercy and truth—because he was in the way.

Eliezer was "just" a servant. We talk a lot about Abraham; hardly anybody talks about Eliezer. Yet it was to this man who remained in the way that God gave this truth, and Eliezer is the first person to declare it to us from the pages of the Word of God. We value fame; God values faithfulness. We value success; God values service. We value applause; God values authenticity. We value recognition; God values righteousness.

You are not going to find out how good God is in one day. Some people say, "Well I tried God." God is not something you try; He is somebody you trust. Are you in the way? Are you in that path that God has for your life? Can you look back and see behind you a well trodden path of faith? When your path is well trodden in the way of God, then God will reveal and manifest His nature to you personally. That is when you will begin to say, "Wow! God your mercy just overwhelms me."

The longer you walk with Him, the more closely you look to Him, the more your own imperfections are magnified. That is the result of understanding God is truth. But, along with that, you discover that this great God loves you in spite of your imperfections, in spite of your failures, in spite of your weaknesses. That is the result of understanding God's mercy.

Eliezer stayed in the way because he had made a commitment. Abraham trusted him with a very difficult assignment. He was to make a long and dangerous journey to find a bride for Isaac. It would have been easy for him to give up. I am sure there were days when he thought about giving up and going home. I imagine he wondered if he had any chance of success at convincing the kind of girl who would be a suitable wife for Isaac to leave her home and family behind to take that long journey back with him. But he has made a vow to Abraham, and he was not going to turn back empty handed.

Eliezer was not afraid of making a commitment. I think many people never really discover who God is because they are so afraid of making commitments to Him. Eliezer was committing himself to a task that, humanly speaking, was impossible. He could not successfully find God's choice of a wife for Isaac without God's help. If the only assignments and tasks that you will take for God are assignments and tasks you can do on your own without His help, you will never discover how merciful and truthful and how great God is. We need to be stretched beyond our comfort zones. That is the only way we can grow. You must make this commitment; God is not going to force you into it.

You will really get to know God in a greater and deeper and personal way by following the example of Eliezer; get in the way and stay there. When you are in the way, follow the leadership of the Lord; He will never lead you wrong. He will never lead you astray. Realize that you are going to have to listen to hear His voice. God does not usually shout. He usually speaks to us in a still, small voice. Eliezer discovered that God is both merciful and truthful because he was committed to remaining in the way.

What impact did this have on Eliezer's life? Notice that in verse 26 it says, *"and the man bowed his head and worshiped the Lord."* When I was younger in the Lord and went to church, we would sing the great songs of faith…"Great is thy faithfulness, Oh God my Father. There is no shadow of turning with Thee. Thou changest not, Thy compassions they fail not…" I loved that song even when I was young, and I would sing every word. But today, after decades of serving God, I cannot sing that song without emotions welling up in my heart and tears coming to my eyes. It is no longer just words on a page in a hymnal. It has become a personal testimony that makes me worship God more and more. I have stayed in the way long enough and by God's grace, He has led me long enough that when I sing "Great is Thy Faithfulness", it is my own experience testifying. There is no substitute for that. Get in the way and stay in the way. Get under God's leadership and follow Him. Never turn to the left. Never turn to the right. You will learn of God's mercy and truth.

Do you know what it means when it says that Eliezer bowed his head? It means his experience absolutely humiliated him. Knowing and understanding God ought to humble us. How dare we stand so arrogantly and wave our fists at God? We do sometimes in our spiritual youth and say, "Oh God, what are you doing to me? You don't care about me at all." How foolish. How childish. Get in the way, stay in the way, follow Him, and you will never say those things again. Because God is absolute mercy and God is absolute truth. Eliezer bowed his head, and he worshiped the Lord.

I wonder, do we really worship the Lord? There is so much talk about worship today. Some people think that unless you are dancing around and playing rock music you aren't worshiping. Other people think that unless you're playing an organ and say "Amen" you aren't worshiping. I think we only really worship the Lord when sincerely out of our own life experience we focus on an aspect of God's character we have discovered and then express that back to Him. That is exactly what Eliezer did. When he worshiped the Lord and he said, "Blessed be the Lord God, the God of my master Abraham who hath not left destitute my master of his mercy and of his truth."

Recently, the senior class of our Christian school took a trip to Scotland and Ireland. It was a very profitable and enjoyable experience. After they got back, several of our young people told me the thing they remembered most from the entire trip was a prayer meeting we took part in at Calvary Church in Magrafeldt. They arrived about an hour before the service was to start and found the people praying. What our young people noticed was that there was a difference between the prayers of the younger Christians and those of the older. The young believers had many burdens on their hearts and they poured their hearts out to God in prayer. But, when the older saints would pray, they could not start asking God for anything without first expressing to Him their worship.

During a similar trip, I had the opportunity to preach with Dr. Ian Paisley of Martyrs Memorial Church in Belfast. We were preaching at a conference north of London; and before the conference, Dr. Paisley met with the other speakers. I appreciate so much that old saint of God, both a pastor and a member of Parliament there for many, many years out of Ulster. This is a man who has suffered greatly for the cause of Christ. That old man put his hand on my shoulder, and he began to pray. As I listened to him extol our great God, I knew I was in the presence of somebody who knew how to worship Him. You do not get that six months after you take up your cross. You do not get that in a decade of going in and out of the way; of being on again, off again. You must stay in the way. You must stay consistent.

Allow the Lord to keep leading you, and eventually something will happen in your heart. You will start discovering things about God that will absolutely overwhelm you. That is what God wants from you and me. He wants us to be overwhelmed with the fact that He is at once absolute mercy and at the same time absolute truth. How do we get there? Eliezer said, "I being in the way the Lord led me."

chapter 2

Do Not Let Mercy & Truth Run Away

My son, forget not my law; but let thine heart keep my commandments: For length of days, and long life, and peace, shall they add to thee. Let not mercy and truth forsake thee: bind them about thy neck; write them upon the table of thine heart: So shalt thou find favour and good understanding in the sight of God and man. –Proverbs 3:1-4

P roverbs is such a wonderful and important book. In a very practical way, it takes the qualities and characteristics of God that we discover in the rest of Scripture and shows us how to apply them to our lives. It teaches us that we ought to desire and achieve wisdom in our lives in order to be like God, who is all wisdom. In this passage from Proverbs, we see that God's mercy and God's truth are to become part of our nature also.

Solomon wrote most of the book of Proverbs, and I can picture him teaching his son Rehoboam these practical truths. We do not know how old Rehoboam was, but Solomon over and over calls him "my son." Solomon knew that Rehoboam would one day be the king of Israel, and he was trying to prepare him for that responsibility; but even more, he was preparing him to live a life that would be pleasing to God. In the evening after court had ended for the day, in the mornings as they took a chariot ride to inspect the troops, in the hot summers when they sat on the veranda of the palace to catch the breeze, Solomon instructed his son in wise living.

When Solomon looked into the eyes of Rehoboam, I believe he saw these two wonderful qualities—mercy and truth—that are so much a part of God's character. Because he said to Rehoboam, *"let not mercy and truth forsake thee,"* it seems that those qualities were already present. When Solomon looked into the eyes of his son, he saw a merciful boy. Rehoboam was kind, he was loving, he was gentle, he was forgiving, and he was generous. So he looked into the eyes of Rehoboam and Solomon said, "Listen son, whatever you do in life, do not allow mercy to depart. Don't let it run away."

But then he also said, "Don't let truth run away either." So, apparently Rehoboam was also an honest son. He was willing to admit when he did wrong, and he was not deceitful. Solomon instructs him to remain transparently honest. "Don't become a deceiver. Don't try and hide the truth. Don't become a liar. Remain committed to discovering God's truth and living by God's truth." You see God is the perfect balance; the perfect blend of mercy and truth. However, these characteristics are not for Him alone. It is God's plan and God's desire for you and me to become men and women of mercy and at the same time men and women of truth.

Rehoboam received excellent advice and instruction from his

father. But let's look at how well he followed it. The Bible tells us in I Kings 11 that Rehoboam became the king of Israel upon the death of his father, Solomon. Many years had passed, and he was a young adult when he assumed the reigns and leadership of the great nation, Israel. I Kings 11:34 says, *"And Solomon slept with his fathers and was buried in the city of his fathers and Rehoboam his son reined in his stead."* This is the same son who received the instruction to forsake not his father's law, to keep his commandments, and to not let mercy and truth run away from him. What happened to him?

And Rehoboam went to Shechem: for all Israel were come to Shechem to make him king. And it came to pass, when Jeroboam the son of Nebat, who was yet in Egypt, heard of it, (for he was fled from the presence of king Solomon, and Jeroboam dwelt in Egypt;) That they sent and called him. And Jeroboam and all the congregation of Israel came, and spake unto Rehoboam, saying, Thy father made our yoke grievous: now therefore make thou the grievous service of thy father, and his heavy yoke which he put upon us lighter, and we will serve thee.

And he said unto them, Depart yet for three days, then come again to me. And the people departed. And king Rehoboam consulted with the old men, that stood before Solomon his father while he yet lived, and said, How do ye advise that I may answer this people? And they spake unto him, saying, If thou wilt be a servant unto this people this day and wilt serve them, and answer them, and speak good words to them, then they will be thy servants for ever.

But he forsook the counsel of the old men, which they had given him, and consulted with the young men that were grown up with him, and which stood before him And he said unto them, What counsel give ye that we may answer this people, who have spoken to me, saying Make the yoke which thy father did put upon us lighter? And the young men that were grown up with him spake unto him, saying, Thus shalt thou speak unto this people that spake unto thee, saying, Thy father made our yoke heavy, but make thou it lighter unto us; thus shalt thou say unto them, My little finger shall be thicker than my father's loins And now whereas my father did lade you with a heavy yoke, I will add to your yoke: my father hath chastised you with whips, but I will chastise you with scorpions.

The people of Israel were wearing a heavy financial yoke, which was a result of Solomon's spiritual decline. Though Solomon was wise, he made the foolish choice to disobey God and marry multiple wives. He needed houses for his 700 wives, and they wanted temples where they could worship their heathen gods. Solomon committed vast amounts of money to support his sinful practices, and the people were forced to pay the price. They asked Rehoboam for relief when he assumed the throne.

Rehoboam received very good advice from his father's counselors, but he did not heed it. He turned his back on the truth they presented to him and did not respond to people with mercy. When he was a young lad, his daddy looked at him and said, "Son do not let mercy and do not let truth forsake you." Where did mercy go? What happened to truth? It was not there any longer. Here was a king aspiring to lead a nation without the balance of both mercy and truth. As a result, he failed miserably. There was a civil war, and there was a division in Israel that never healed. Generations far into the future suffered because of Rehoboam's unwillingness to maintain mercy and truth in balance in his leadership and in his personal life. Rehoboam is a sad example of how absolutely imperative it is that we maintain the balance between mercy and truth.

There is a tendency for us to allow mercy or truth to run away and not go after them. You see there's something about mercy and truth that they want to run away, because mercy and truth generally do not like each other. If you were to personify mercy and personify truth, they mix like oil and water. God said to Solomon, to Rehoboam, and to every one of us that we must always maintain mercy and always maintain truth. But truth is critical of mercy. Truth says, "Mercy, you're weak. Mercy, you don't understand. If everything's left to you, it's going to fall apart. You can't just stroke people and pat them or everything's going to fall apart. They need a good dose of the truth." On the other hand, mercy says, "Yes, but without me, you'd be harsh and drive people away." The problem is that most people let one or the other depart. Generally, the one that departs is the one that is our weakness.

Even though they are polar opposites, both mercy and truth in their purest essence are spiritual gifts from God. When you study Romans 12 and I Corinthians 12, you will see that God gifts some people with an inordinate amount of mercy. But then, you have others who are filled with truth. In fact, the twenty-three times that these two are talked about directly, they always come in the same order: mercy and truth. It is as if God is saying, "All right truth we need you, but not until mercy gets here first!" Parents need this balance. If truth is allowed to dominate and mercy is subdued, then there is the potential of incredible rebellion in the lives of our children. If mercy overcomes truth, they will grow up without a commitment to doing right and staying within God's boundaries.

The commitment to keep mercy and truth is not a decision that is made just once in your life. Rehoboam had them once, but he let them run away. This is something you will have to come back to regularly. Knowing that, what can we do? How can we remain in balance between mercy and truth? Solomon said to Rehoboam, *"Bind them* [mercy and truth] *about thy neck."* God views mercy and truth as beautiful ornaments to be worn; like putting on a beautiful piece of jewelry for a woman. In the morning, when you get up, you put on the ornaments, the beautiful necklaces, as it were, of mercy and of truth. You know if a lady has on a beautiful broach or a beautiful necklace or ring. There is something that attracts your attention to it. Here is what God is saying: if you want to be a beautiful, attractive Christian, then you adorn yourself every day with mercy and truth. Make the decision to be kind and generous and gentle and good and forgiving. Make the commitment to be honest and faithful and truthful. Put on both.

This is the key to effective parenting. It is the key to effective leadership. It is the key to effective preaching. We must have the balance between mercy and truth. Most of the problems that we have are caused when we lose our balance. Solomon also told Rehoboam, *"Write them* [mercy and truth] *upon the table of thine heart.*" In Bible times, writing on tables or tablets referred to carving something in stone. It was something that would never be changed or forgotten. That is how important keeping mercy and truth is.

My son, keep thy father's commandment, and forsake not the law of thy mother: Bind them continually upon thine heart, and tie them about thy neck. When thou goest, it shall lead thee; when thou sleepest, it shall keep thee; and when thou awakest, it shall talk with thee. For the commandment is a lamp; and the law is light; and reproofs of instruction are the way of life: To keep thee from the evil woman, from the flattery of the tongue of a strange woman. Proverbs 6:20-24

The idea we see here is that maintaining mercy and truth offers us protection. It keeps us from evil as we navigate through life. Mercy and truth are vitally important as we interact with others, but they are also vitally important as we walk with God day by day. Notice the two analogies God uses—an outward, adorning necklace, and an inward tablet within our heart. Mercy and truth are for both our outward and inward relationships. I have often seen this happen: Someone hears this teaching on mercy and truth and depending what their strength or weakness is says, "God I'm just not as strong in mercy as I ought to be. Help me to be more merciful." But in a few days, they have forgotten all about it and are back to the same old self. This balance cannot be maintained just externally; it must also become part of our character.

If you are like me, you are probably thinking, "I don't have that ability. Oh, I can do the mercy part with my hands tied behind my back, but that truth part…" Or you may be saying,

"Well, that truth part comes pretty easy to me, but that mercy part…" Yet God says we must write both on the table of our hearts. It's a commitment that you and I have to make. The good news is that God doesn't expect us to write them on the table of our hearts by ourselves. Jeremiah 31:33 says, *"But this shall be the covenant that I will make with the house of Israel; After those days, saith the Lord, I will put my law in their inward parts, and write it in their hearts; and will be their God and they shall be my people."* A covenant is an agreement between two people. Part of God's agreement with us is that He will join with us in the process of shaping and developing our character.

Yes, we have a responsibility. Solomon told Rehoboam to write. But, God also says He will write. I want to be a balanced Christian with both mercy and truth, but to save my soul I can't etch them in my character. I can't change me; but what I can do is I can say, "God, I can't change me, but You can etch it in my character. Would You help me?" I write it, but God writes it through me. Here's what he does: He puts His hand over mine, and then when the writing is done, the etching of God's qualities in our character is a result of God's hand on my hand. If you are going to have eternal change in your character, it will not happen by trying harder. You are only going to get it by the God putting His hand over your hand and etching His character into your nature. Put the welcome mat out and bring mercy and truth back into your life. You can put them on as an ornament; but more than that, you can have them in your heart. This same principle is not only found in Old Testament, but in the New Testament as well.

Do we begin again to commend ourselves? Or need we, as some others, epistles of commendation to you, or letters of commendation from you? Ye are our epistle written in our hearts, known and read of all men: Forasmuch as ye are manifestly declared to be the epistle of Christ ministered by us, written not with ink, but with the Spirit of the living God; not in tables of stone, but in fleshy tables of the heart."
2 Corinthians 3:1-3

By the way, that's the 67th book in the Bible—you! Paul by inspiration said that you are the epistles of God. I cannot change my character. I cannot etch mercy and truth in my heart, but as I make covenant with God, God's hand goes over mine. God uses the ink; He uses the writing instrument of His Holy Spirit to etch His character on my nature. Paul said it's not ink; it's the Holy Spirit of God. You see, when you become a person of mercy and you become a person of truth, when it truly becomes a part of your character, you cannot say, "Well you know it was because of me." No! You have to say, "It was because of God's hand on mine. It was because of the ink of the Holy Spirit of God that this was etched into my character. I am a new man now. I am not the same way I used to be. I am not so imbalanced. I am not so ineffective. Now God is bringing me to a place of a completeness in mercy and completeness in truth, so that I can maximize my potential and effectiveness in every part of my life." That is the result of maintaining mercy and truth. *"So shalt thou find favor and good understanding in the sight of God and man."* (Proverbs 3:4)

chapter 3

The Mother of Mercy & Truth

My son, forget not my law; but let thine heart keep my commandments:
For length of days, and long life, and peace, shall they add to thee. Let
not mercy and truth forsake thee: bind them about thy neck; write
them upon the table of thine heart: So shalt thou find favour and
good understanding in the sight of God and man.—Proverbs 3:1-4

We have looked at this passage from the standpoint of the lesson Solomon taught to his son, but now I want us to look at it from the standpoint of Solomon himself. Where did he learn the importance of the balance between mercy and truth? How did he know this doctrine needed to be shared with his son? I believe much of this teaching can be traced back to Solomon's mother, Bathsheba. Of course you know the story of David and Bathsheba and their illicit relationship when she was married to Uriah. She became pregnant, and David tried to cover his sin. He eventually had her husband murdered and married Bathsheba. It looked like he had successfully hidden his sin, but God revealed it.

Nathan the prophet came and told David the story about the man who had one little sheep who lived next to a man who had the great flocks. The man with the great flocks stole the little sheep of the other man. David was infuriated and pronounced judgment on him, but then Nathan said, "You're the man! You stole another man's wife, and you had relations with her. Now, she's with your child!" Consequently, the child died; but then later, God gave to David and Bathsheba, Solomon. Look at how Solomon describes his relationship with his mother.

Hear, ye children, the instruction of a father, and attend to know understanding. For I give you good doctrine, forsake ye not my law. For I was my father's son, tender and only beloved in the sight of my mother. Proverbs 4:1-3

Though Solomon's mother had been in Heaven for many years by the time Proverbs was written, his memories of her mercy and truth were etched vividly in his memory. This passage in particular focuses on her mercy. In remembering his mother, Bathsheba, he said, "In my relationship with her when I was tender, my mother made me feel as if I was only beloved in her sight." Now, this is an incredible statement of mercy. The word "tender" is describing the time in a person's life from conception until about twenty years of age. In the Hebrew culture when a young man or young woman turned twenty, they were responsible and accountable as an adult. So, the tender years are the formative years of life. When Solomon reminisced about his mother, he said, "I remember growing up in the home of the king. I remember my mother and how during those tender years she made me feel as if I was only beloved in her sight." Specifically, what the word 'only beloved' means has behind it the idea as exclusively united as if he were an only child. An only child can get 100% of the love and tenderness and affection and mercy and goodness of his mother.

The interesting thing is that Solomon was not an only child. We know from I Chronicles 3:5 that Bathsheba also bore three more children; Shimea, Shobab and Nathan. Isn't it amazing that David and Bathsheba named one of their children after the very prophet of God who came and confronted David with his sin? So, Solomon was not an only child, but he said, "My mother made me feel so special as if I were an only child. The literal meaning of the word "beloved" is exclusively united. And the expression "in the sight of" actually has behind it in the Hebrew the idea of her face against my face. There is something tender and merciful about cuddling and holding a little child in your arms. That is what Solomon had in his memory when he reflected on his childhood.

He said, "I remember a mother who, though there were other children in the family, made me feel so special. She made me feel as if I were her exclusive child. It was as if we were cheek to cheek, face-to-face. There was a relationship that I had with my mother that was close and intimate, and it was because of my mother's great mercy her kindness and goodness that she had." When you think about all that Bathsheba had gone through, she could have been very, very bitter. She could have been angry at David. She could have been bitter and angry at God. She could have looked at Solomon and been reminded about the child that God had caused to die and allowed those disappointments and discouraging events out of her past to control her life. So, why wasn't she bitter? Why did she fill Solomon's tender years with mercy?

I think the key is found in Solomon's names. He actually had three. Solomon was his official family name, given to him by David when he was born. Solomon means peaceable. David viewed this baby as a token of the peace he had gained with God through repentance, and I believe of the peace he had gained with Bathsheba. But, if you read Second Samuel 12:24 and 25, we find that they sent the birth announcement to the prophet Nathan, and asked for a blessing name. Nathan said, "Name him Jedediah. Jedediah means beloved of the Lord. What a wonderful statement for this man of God to make! But on top of that, his mother also gave him a nickname. In Proverbs 31, he says that his mother called him Lemuel. Lemuel means one who belongs to God.

Every parent needs this understanding. Our children are given to us by God, but they still belong to Him. I believe this name that Bathsheba used for Solomon was an expression of her acceptance of God's decision to take her firstborn child from her arms and transport that little child's soul and spirit to Heaven. She recognized her responsibility as a mother; and rather than neglecting it, she took it very seriously. She invested herself unselfishly into the life of this child because she understood that he belonged to God. A second passage shows us that in addition to mercy, Bathsheba was characterized by truth.

The words of king Lemuel, the prophecy that his mother taught him. Proverbs 31:1

The word prophecy here is the Bible expression for a bold

declaration of God's truth. In the Old Testament, the prophets brought God's Word to His people. They had very little written Scripture, and only a few people would have had the opportunity to read the words of Moses written by inspiration of God. Therefore, the prophets would declare God's messages to the nation of Israel. Prophesying was not just done by men in the pulpit. It was also accomplished by fathers and mothers who were committed to rearing children in the truth. And, Bathsheba was such a mother. Solomon, in reminiscing about her said, "Oh yeah, momma was sweet and kind and good, but I want to tell you momma could preach every bit as good as the old prophet, Nathan."

The word Solomon used for "taught" is very interesting. It is not talking about a teacher in front of a classroom. It is a "correction" word. It is the idea of chastening or chastising someone until they change their behavior. I have heard people refer to a paddle as the "board of education," and that is exactly what Solomon is saying here about his mother's instruction. Yes, she had mercy; but she also had truth. There is a vivid illustration of this balance in action found at the end of David's life, when Solomon was supposed to be placed upon the throne found in First Kings chapter 1.

David had many other sons beside Solomon, and several of them wanted to be king. David named Solomon as his heir, but rather than accept that, Adonijah tried to grab the throne for himself. As we walk through this story, watch as Bathsheba shows both mercy and truth as she interacts with David. David was seventy years of age. That is not terribly old, but David had had a hard life filled with battles. The years had taken a toll on him, and he had become very feeble. Because of David's condition, his advisors in the kingdom had a beauty contest to find one of the most beautiful virgins in the land. (This was not a good idea, and it would come back to cause more trouble for Solomon later on, but it is what they did.) They found Abishag the Shunammite and brought her to David. She moved in with the king to take care of him, and the queen moved out. This had to have been difficult for Bathsheba to endure. But there was something worse for her to deal with. Adonijah rebelled against David's plan of succession. Bathsheba knew that if he became king, the first thing he would do would be to kill Solomon.

Why was Adonijah so rebellious? He did not receive both mercy and truth. First Kings 1:6 says, *"And his father had not displeased him at any time in saying, Why has thou done so? And he also was a very goodly man; and his mother bare him after Absalom."* What an indictment against David. David was filled with mercy for his children, but David could never bring himself to confront them with the truth. David was a great warrior, but David was an awful father. Adonijah's becoming a rebel was directly contributed to by his father's unwillingness to displease him in anything. Whatever he wanted, David gave him.

Bathsheba had a wonderful influence on her husband in this regard. Though David failed miserably with his earlier children, I believe it was Bathsheba who helped him see the importance of adding truth to his mercy. We looked at Proverbs 4:3 and saw Bathsheba's mercy toward Solomon, but the next verse says, "he (David) taught me…" The David who reared Solomon was not the same man who failed with Adonijah, Absalom, and Amnon. Because of the influence of Bathsheba in David's life, he took personal interest in becoming a man of mercy and a man of truth. He was committed, even though he had failed miserably with his other children, to raising this child for God. That is the power of influence that a mother and a wife can have on her husband.

When God made Adam; He made him needing somebody else. That somebody else was Eve. Wife, you are that somebody else for your husband. You can have influence on your husband to correct his imbalances. If you are faithful, you can actually see him transformed and conformed and grow to become wiser and better. If he needs to be merciful, he can become more merciful. If he needs to become more truthful, he can become more truthful. Bathsheba came into David's life, and she simply lived with him committed to mercy and committed to truth, and David made a change. Sometimes, we point fingers at others saying, "They ought to be this, or they ought to be that; they ought to do this, or they ought to do that." But, we forget that we have the power of influence on them. And now, at the end of his life, Bathsheba is once again going to display mercy and truth toward David.

Adonijah has announced that he is going to become king. First Kings 1:15 says, *"And Bathsheba went in unto the king into the chamber: and the king was very old; and Abishag the Shunammite ministered unto the king."* When Bathsheba went to David, she had to confront this young woman who had replaced her. The role of being with her husband and caring for his needs had been taken over by someone else. Any godly woman would have a difficult time in such a situation. This was awkward. Yet, Bathsheba demonstrated great mercy. Verse 16 says, *"And Bathsheba bowed, and did obeisance unto the king,"* That is mercy. It would have been easy for Bathsheba to get focused on what her husband was doing wrong and get focused on this Abishag that was now in his life.

But, if she had become so focused on the hurt of that, she would have missed out on her responsibility to communicate truth to her husband in this critical time in their nation's history. The next time that you are tempted to get upset with something that is happening in your life, instead stop and think that God may be putting you in a situation where you could have a profound influence for good. You may lose that opportunity unless you exercise mercy and keep your mouth shut about that problem. Bathsheba showed mercy by what she didn't say and what she didn't do. She also remained focused on truth. She told her husband what apparently none of his other advisors were willing to tell him. "David, your son Adonijah has just proclaimed himself king. You told Solomon that he would become the king." She could not do anything else about Adonijah's rebellion and his threat to her son's life, but mercy and truth together were enough. David responded to her request and made the arrangements to ensure Solomon became the king.

A mother filled with mercy and truth, not only has the potential to influence profoundly her own husband, to see him changed as Bathsheba did with David, but she also has the potential to help her children maximize their potential in this world. Solomon was destined to be a king, but if he had not had a mother who was filled with mercy and truth, who handled herself wisely and discreetly, Solomon's potential would never have been realized. Adonijah would have become king, and Solomon would have been killed. Never underestimate the power of a woman, a mother who is filled with mercy and at the same time filled with truth.

chapter 4

The Quality of Mercy

And when the morning arose, then the angels hastened Lot, saying, Arise, take thy wife, and thy two daughters, which are here; lest thou be consumed in the iniquity of the city. And while he lingered the men laid hold upon his hand, and upon the hand of his wife, and upon the hand of his two daughters; The Lord being merciful unto him: and they brought him forth, and set him without the city, and it came to pass, when they had brought them forth abroad, that he said, Escape for thy life; look not behind thee, neither stay thou in all the plain; escape to the mountain, lest thou be consumed. And Lot said unto them, Oh, not so, my Lord: Behold now, thy servant hath found grace in thy sight, and thou hast magnified thy mercy, which thou hast shewed unto me in saving my life; and I cannot escape to the mountain, lest some evil take me, and I die:"–Genesis 19:15-19

So far we have looked at the importance of maintaining the balance between mercy and truth. Now, we are going to look specifically at mercy—what it is, and why and how mercy can forsake us. To help us understand both of these questions, we are going to look back at Genesis to the place where mercy is first mentioned in the Bible. As is so often true, when Genesis 19 talks about mercy, it is talking about God's mercy. Every good quality begins with God and reflects His perfect nature. He is the best, the epitome, the fullness of every good characteristic and quality. The simplest definition of mercy is that it is God's kindness given to us.

Genesis 19 shows us God's mercy in the life of Lot, Abraham's nephew. Lot came out of Ur along with Abraham. For many years, he lived with his uncle, but by the time of Genesis 19, Lot was living in the middle of a city called Sodom. Along with its companion city Gomorrah, Sodom was a wicked, wicked city. As this story from the life of Lot unfolds, Sodom and Gomorrah are about to be utterly and completely destroyed. Because of God's mercy, He first sent some messengers, some angels to the city to Lot's house to warn him to flee the city before it was destroyed. But, Lot was attached to Sodom. He and his family did not want to leave; they "lingered." In fact, the angels had to literally drag them out of town to get them to go. Lot certainly did not deserve mercy, but he received it.

The word for "merciful" here is also translated "to spare." In others words, though Lot was deserving of certain consequences for his actions, God spared him. You also need to be a person filled with mercy. You do not always have to exact the consequences when somebody does something that is wrong. Mercy is compassion in action. Mercy says, "You have done wrong. You deserve these consequences, but I'm not going to give you what you deserve." That is mercy. Notice that our passage of Scripture tells us that Lot recognized the mercy he had received. He thanked God for sparing his life and his daughters' lives from destruction. Mercy is never deserved. It is only granted because of the nature and character of the giver, not the recipient.

Lot made a distinction between grace and mercy; they are not two words for the same thing. Mercy keeps us from getting what we deserve. Grace gives us what we do not deserve. It is only God's mercy that extends His grace to save us and keep us from eternity in Hell. The Bible says that it is by God's mercy that we are not all consumed every day (Lam. 3:22). God says, "Because of My mercy I choose not to exact the consequences that you have coming. That's My mercy. Now, My grace takes you a step further. Not only are you not going to hell; My grace opens up Heaven to you." What an amazing gift! But Lot's story tells us more than just what mercy is; it also tells us why mercy forsakes people.

We see a contrast here between Divine mercy and our mercy. When Lot talked about how God "magnified" His mercy, he is talking about God increasing mercy. If there was ever someone who needed God's increased mercy, it was Lot. He left the place of blessing with his uncle Abraham and pitched his tents toward Sodom. He moved into the city and was accepted by those evil men. He even went so far as to offer up his own daughters to the angry mob besieging his house. And when the angels tried to warn him to flee, they literally had to drag him out of the city to save his life. Lot's sinful stubbornness needed increased mercy!

We only have so much mercy; and when we run out of it, we say, "You're just going to get it. You deserve it; your comeuppance and that's it." And we can do that. But, when God saw Lot, He magnified Himself and said, "I'm just not going to do that, I'm going to magnify my mercy. I'm just going to make it bigger."

Somewhere along the way in every relationship you have, your mercy is going to run out. At that point, you have two choices. You can decide that you have done enough in behalf of that individual and say, "Well, they've crossed the line now." The problem with that approach is from then on you have absolutely no spiritual influence in their lives. Or, you can say, "My mercy needs to be magnified. It needs to grow. God increase my mercy so that it doesn't run out." When you do not want to give it, you magnify it, and you give it anyway. Lot did some hideous things. Yet, God magnified His mercy. When we draw the line and we say "no more mercy" without consulting God, we eliminate the possibility of any kind of ministry to that person ever again. That's why the Bible says, "Let not mercy forsake thee."

Lot really did not even want God's mercy. He refused to leave Sodom. We might say, "If I were God, I wouldn't be grabbing their hand and pulling them out." But, God did because He will not let mercy forsake Him. He could say, "I don't want to be merciful to you. I don't feel like being merciful to you. I feel like giving you your comeuppance, and you deserve it. That's exactly how I feel, but I'm not going to do it. I'm going to magnify My mercy. I'm just going to let My mercy grow." Though Lot continually failed, God continually magnified His mercy. Mercy attempts to forsake us when someone continually flaunts the mercy that has been extended to them again and again and again. God magnified His mercy over and over again to Lot. And, through His grace and the power of His Holy Spirit you can magnify mercy toward others, just as God magnifies it toward you.

So, how can we keep mercy from forsaking us? When we want to say good riddance and do not feel like being merciful, how do we keep mercy? To answer that question, we have to understand why God was so merciful to Lot. It had nothing to do with Lot; it had everything to do with God's relationship with Abraham. In Genesis chapter 18, God came down to talk with Abraham.

And the men rose up from thence, and looked toward Sodom: and Abraham went with them to bring them on the way. And the Lord said, Shall I hide from Abraham that thing which I do; Seeing that Abraham shall surely become a great and mighty nation, and all the nations of the earth shall be blessed in him? For I know him, that he will command his children and his household after him, and they shall keep the way of the Lord, to do justice and judgment; that the Lord may bring upon Abraham that which he hath spoken of him. And the Lord said, Because the cry of Sodom and Gomorrah is great, and because their sin is very grievous: I will go down now, and see whether they have done altogether according to the cry of it, which is come unto me; and if not, I will know. And the men turned their faces from thence, and went toward Sodom: but Abraham stood yet before the Lord. And Abraham drew near, and said, Wilt thou also destroy the righteous with the wicked? Genesis 18:16-23

Abraham interceded on behalf of Lot. He "bargained" God

all the way down to ten righteous people. It is sad to realize that if Lot had just won his own family, the entire city would have been spared. But, there were not ten righteous people in Sodom. So, the basis of God's mercy to Lot was not the bargaining that He did with Abraham; it was because of God's love, respect, and appreciation for Abraham. God said, "Abraham, because you care for Lot, because you want me to be merciful to Lot, I'm going to be merciful. I'm all done with him. I'm ready to let him burn up, but I'm going to be merciful to him again. Not because of who he is, not because of what he's doing, but I'm going to be merciful to him because of My relationship with you, Abraham." This is precisely the way that we can keep mercy in our lives. It is not on the basis of the other person's behavior; it is on the basis of our relationship with the Lord.

When my relationship is right with the Lord, then I can have the mercy that I need to magnify mercy. Because God has extended incredible mercy to me, I can then turn and give that same mercy to others. But, if I am not in a right relationship with God, I forget why I received His mercy. God's mercy toward me is not because of who I am or anything good that I have done, but because of His relationship with His Son—and His Son loves me. Ephesians 4:32 says, *"even as God for Christ's sake hath forgiven you."* That is the whole foundation of mercy. Do you know how important those three words 'for Christ's sake' are? God did not forgive you for your sake; He forgave you for Christ's sake. He did not forgive you because you are someone special. He forgave you because His Son is Someone special, and His Son has an eye for you. His Son loves you. If you are in a right relationship with the Son of God, and you are experiencing the favor and mercy of God as a result of that relationship with the Son of God, then and only then can you have the mercy that you need to turn and extend mercy to somebody else who does not deserve mercy.

We tend to write some people off as not deserving of mercy. Lot was a mess. He failed with his uncle, he failed with his wife, and he failed greatly with his daughters. He did not heed the warnings of God. He failed to be a witness to those around him. If there were anyone we would think of as not deserving mercy, it would be Lot. I have heard people say things like, "Preacher, after what he did to me, I don't even think he's saved!" Well, if all we knew about Lot was what is in Genesis, I would not think he was saved either...but that is not the whole story. Second Peter 2:7 recounts the events of Genesis 19 and says God "delivered just Lot." That expression "just" means that Lot was a believer; he was a saved man. Before you judge someone as not deserving of mercy, you need to see them the way God sees them. God gave Lot mercy because He could see some things in Lot that others did not see. When you are not the person making the decision to extend mercy or not, do not try to be God. The only one who can see it all is God. Before we cut off mercy to someone, we have a responsibility to get a thorough understanding of that person and where they are in their lives.

Over the years, I have found that God is willing to go way beyond what I am willing to do in this matter of mercy with people. What did God see when He looked at Lot? Second Peter

2:8&9 says, *"(For that righteous man dwelling among them, in seeing and hearing, vexed his righteous soul from day to day with their unlawful deeds ;) the Lord knoweth how to deliver the godly out of temptations..."* God saw a righteous godly man who had damaged himself by the decisions he had made. He saw a man who had strayed far from the path of righteousness. He saw a man whose values and heart had been turned toward the things of the world. And, God saw a man who needed mercy.

By God's grace, attempt to see the bigger picture in people's lives. Look beyond today, look beyond the hurt, look beyond the sin, and see that God can still do a great and mighty work in them. They have made bad decisions (but so have you!) We have all made bad decisions. God gave us mercy. He gives us mercy, and He continues to give us mercy. We do not know the full story, but God does. Therefore, we ought to be very, very careful before we cut off mercy to someone. You better be sure that that is what God is calling for, because when you cut it off there is no more future opportunity. You are going to reach a point where you will say, "I don't want to be kind anymore. I don't want to be benevolent. I don't want to be good. I want to forsake mercy and give them what they have coming." But, God will magnify your mercy. Look at the bigger picture of his life. Look at the bigger picture of her life. If you maintain mercy, you maximize the possibility of bringing that person back to a personal relationship with Christ that's dynamic and real and a personal relationship with you. That is what mercy does.

In William Shakespeare's famous play, *The Merchant of Venice,*

Shylock the moneylender insists on claiming his "pound of flesh," when Antonio defaults on his loan. Such a judgment that would certainly kill Antonio since the flesh was to be taken directly over his heart. Portia, Shylock's daughter asks for mercy with these famous words:

The quality of mercy is not strain'd,
It droppeth as the gentle rain from heaven
Upon the place beneath. It is twice blest:
It blesseth him that gives and him that takes.

Show mercy to those around you—it will be a blessing to both you and them. And, as Jesus said in the Beatitudes, when you are merciful, you will be called "children of God."

chapter 5

How the Son of the Morning Became the Father of Lies

How art thou fallen from heaven O Lucifer, son of the morning! How art thou cut down to the ground which didst weaken the nations. –Isaiah 14:12

Ye are of your father the devil and the lusts of your father ye will do. He was a murderer from the beginning and abode not in the truth because there's no truth in him. When he speaketh a lie, he speaketh of his own, for he is a liar and the father of It.–John 8:44

We have looked at the warning in Proverbs 3 to not let mercy and truth forsake us. I want to use the story of the fall of Lucifer to illustrate for you what happens when we do not keep the truth. Lucifer went from being the "son of the morning" to becoming the "father of lies." This is a startling and vivid picture of the danger of losing the truth. Before God created the world, He made the angels. Above all the angels were three archangels—Michael, Gabriel, and Lucifer. Each of these glorious beings had a responsibility to lead other angels in praise and worship and service to God. When God named them, He picked names with meaning. Michael means "who is like God?" Gabriel means "strong man of God." And Lucifer means "light-bringer." God called him the "son of the morning" or a morning star, which is very significant because that is one of the names of Jesus. (Revelation 22:16) Although we do not know for certain because the Scripture does not tell us, it may be that each one of the archangels was associated particularly with one member of the Trinity, and that Lucifer was the angel who most closely worked with Jesus Christ. Yet, this incredible creature of brightness and honor and integrity ended up as the father of all lies because he let truth forsake him.

We are still dealing with Lucifer's loss of trustworthiness, loss of transparent honesty, loss of integrity and character, and the sin he brought into the world through Adam even today. The repercussions of the absence of truth in a person's life last far into the future. Before you give up truth, I want you to consider the consequences of dishonesty, the consequences of lying, the consequences of deceiving others, the consequences of playing the life of a hypocrite. It will destroy everything good and beautiful in your life. And, you will not be able to limit the fallout—allowing the truth to flee from you will damage your family and those around you, perhaps for many generations to come. If leaving the truth could so transform Lucifer, never forget what it will do to you.

If truth forsakes you, you are already on the way to a destiny of destruction. This drastic transformation is not just limited to the Devil—it will happen in your life if you let truth run away. I have counseled women who married what they thought was a man of integrity and honesty and transparency. Perhaps he once was, just as the devil was at one time. Now, things have changed. They weep and ask, "How did this man become such a monster? Where did it go wrong?" How many parents have caught their children in absolute deception and been totally shocked. "I can't believe this is my son; this is my daughter. What in the world happened to my child?" Thousands of people trusted Bernie Madoff with their life savings. He was so trusted that for many years he was the head of the NASDAQ stock exchange. Yet, more than fifty billion dollars vanished into his web of deception and dishonesty.

What happened to Satan can also happen to you. You can lie so many times that you cannot tell the truth anymore. You lie to yourself and you lie to others until you do not even recognize that you are lieing. Many a man and woman of character have forfeited integrity and honesty as the truth forsook them. The question then is what happened to Lucifer to so transform him. The answer is found in Isaiah 14.

For thou hast said in thine heart, I will ascend into heaven, I will exalt my throne above the stars of God: I will sit also upon the mount of the congregation, in the sides of the north: I will ascend above the heights of the clouds; I will be like the most High. Isaiah 14:13&14

Notice that his problem started in his heart. The loss of truth, the loss of honesty, the loss of integrity always starts there. The person who trusts his heart is incredibly foolish. Why? Because your heart is deceitful above all things, the Bible says, and desperately wicked. (Jeremiah 17:9) You cannot follow your heart. You can follow the word of God. To keep the truth, we must follow what God leads us to do by His Spirit and by His Word. Notice the five statements Lucifer made:

1. **I will** ascend into heaven.
2. **I will** exalt my throne above the stars of God.
3. **I will** sit also upon the mount of the congregation in the sides in the north.
4. **I will** ascend above the height of the clouds.
5. **I will** be like the most High.

Now what is, "I will"? It is a statement of ambition. Now, ambition is a wonderful blessing. It is a part of the character of God; and because we were made in God's image, we have ambition as well. He puts within us a desire to better ourselves, a desire to move forward, a desire to achieve. The problem comes when ambition goes awry. All sin is an aberration or a distortion of something that God made good.

The morning star became the father of lies when his ambition went awry. Ambition is a necessary ingredient in life, so when Lucifer said, "I will ascend" that in and of itself is not wrong. Ambition is a good thing. You ought to want to be better. Ambition leads us to advancement. Secondly, he said, "I will exalt my throne." Do you know what he wanted? Lucifer wanted to be approved, admired, and accepted. One of the things that make ambition such a strong force is the desire to be accepted and find approval. Again, it is not a bad thing unless we allow that to be twisted.

No one was more ambitious for God than Lucifer. By the way, he took that ambition with him when he fell. Nobody is more ambitious for evil today than Lucifer. He is at it 24/7, seven days a week, 365 days a year trying to get people to do wrong. The third statement that Lucifer made was, "I will sit also up on the mount of the congregation on the sides of the North." It is a terrible thing to declare ourselves equal with God. But, at the same time, a desire for authority is not necessarily wrong. In First Timothy 3:1 Paul said that desiring to be a pastor was the desire for a "good work." The determining factor is the reason why we want authority—is it for control or to help others? Godly leadership springs out of ambition. There should be something within you that says, "I want to be useful as a leader."

His fourth statement was, "I will ascend above the heights." This is a great desire to be the best that you can be in your field. There is never a reason for a child of God to settle for less than that. God wants us to achieve the best that we can. When Moses was inspired by his father-in-law, Jethro, to select men from among the children of Israel for leadership positions so he would not get worn out with everyone coming to him with their problems, the Bible says he chose them according to their ability. Some could lead ten. Some could lead a hundred. Some could lead a thousand. Some could lead ten thousand. It does not mean that any man was less important than another. It simply acknowledges that our achievement level is not going to be exactly the same. The Bible forbids us to compare ourselves among ourselves. (II Cor. 10:12)

The only acceptable standard for my achievement is what God has for me. Lucifer wan an incredible leader who was once filled with good ambition.

Finally he said, "I will be like the most High." My one consuming desire is to be like Christ. Paul said that God's ultimate plan and purpose for our lives is that we be conformed to the image of His Son. (Romans 8:29) I am ambitious about being like Jesus. But, ambition can be taken in a wrong direction, and that is exactly what happened to Lucifer. How did his ambition go awry? First, Lucifer's "I will" was not exercised within the circle of God's will. James talked about people who were ambitious to build their business and plan for the future but did not consider God's purposes in their thinking.

Go to now, ye that say, To day or to morrow we will go into such a city, and continue there a year, and buy and sell, and get gain: Whereas ye know not what shall be on the morrow. For what is your life? It is even a vapour, that appeareth for a little time, and then vanisheth away. For that ye ought to say, If the Lord will, we shall live, and do this, or that. James 4:13-15

What we ought to say is, "I want to do this. I've got ambition. I want to advance. I want to be appreciated. I want authority so that I might lead. I want to be the best that I can be. I want to be like the Lord." That is a great and wonderful ambition because it is bounded first and foremost by what God's will is. Lucifer's statements of, "I will" were completely oblivious to God's will. When our will is exercised inside of God's will, it leads to advancement, to excitement, to achievement, to greatness, and to success. The moment you and I step outside of the parameters of God's will for our lives, we fall. Our ambition turns against us and the truth forsakes us. That is what happened to Lucifer.

By contrast, look at the example of Christ in the Garden of Gethsemane. He knew that He was facing Calvary, facing the bearing of our sins, facing His Father turning His back on Him. In His prayer in the Garden, we see Christ exercising His will inside of the will of His Father. *"He went a little further and fell on his face and prayed, O God my father, if it be possible let this cup pass from me* (that's His will, but He doesn't stop there). *Nevertheless, not as I will, but as thou will."* (Matt. 26:39) You see, we can stay within the parameters of God's will and exercise our ambition as long as we are content within God's will. As long as Lucifer did that, he soared successfully. That is true for us as well; but the moment we violate His will by a lack of submission to His will in favor of our will, we step outside of those parameters. That places us on dangerous ground. We can be ambitious as God leads us, and we should be; but we also need to maintain the attitude Jesus had, "nevertheless, not my will, but Thine be done."

What led Lucifer, who enjoyed all of this wonderful glory, all of this amazing opportunity to honor and glorify God, to step out of submission to God's will? The answer is found in Ezekiel 28. Like Isaiah 14, this is also a parallel passage, which means it is talking about a human being but at the same time talking about the demise and destruction of Satan.

Son of man, take up a lamentation upon the king of Tyrus, and say unto him, Thus saith the Lord GOD; Thou sealest up the sum, full of wisdom, and perfect in beauty. Thou hast been in Eden the garden of God; every precious stone was thy covering, the sardius, topaz, and the diamond, the beryl, the onyx, and the jasper, the sapphire, the emerald, and the carbuncle, and gold: the workmanship of thy tabrets and of thy pipes was prepared in thee in the day that thou wast created. Thou art the anointed cherub that covereth; and I have set thee so: thou wast upon the holy mountain of God; thou hast walked up and down in the midst of the stones of fire. Thou wast perfect in thy ways from the day that thou wast created, till iniquity was found in thee. Ezekiel 28:12-15

What a sad transition! Lucifer went from being full of wisdom and perfect in beauty to being filled with iniquity. What happened? Ezekiel 28:17 says, *"Thine heart was lifted up because of thy beauty. Thou hast corrupted thy wisdom by reason of thy brightness."* The thing that destroyed Lucifer was pride. He was filled with pride over his own achievements, his own abilities, his own accomplishments, and his own God-given nature. The success that Lucifer achieved within God's rules and God's will led him to believe that he did not need God. He forgot that everything he had was a result of God's design.

That began the decision making process to take his ambition and extend it outside of God's will; and when that happened, Lucifer lost his integrity. If we allow pride to grow in our hearts, we will lose our integrity also. Every good thing that you have and every good thing that you do is a direct result of the goodness and grace of Almighty God. In his first letter to the church at Corinth, Paul made this point very clear.

And these things, brethren, I have in a figure transferred to myself and to Apollos for your sakes; that ye might learn in us not to think of men above that which is written, that no one of you be puffed up for one against another. For who maketh thee to differ from another? and what hast thou that thou didst not receive? now if thou didst receive it, why dost thou glory, as if thou hadst not received it? I Corinthians 4:6&7

The loss of truth from your life and the horrible consequences that follow begin when your ambition is twisted and you start taking credit for accomplishments and achievements that ultimately belong to God. That is how the son of the morning became the father of lies. And it will devastate your life if you do not guard against it.

chapter 6

A One-Legged Man Cannot Run

My son, forget not my law; but let thine heart keep my commandments: For length of days, and long life, and peace, shall they add to thee. Let not mercy and truth forsake thee: bind them about thy neck; write them upon the table of thine heart: So shalt thou find favour and good understanding in the sight of God and man. Proverbs 3:1-4

God designed the world to be in balance. At the very beginning of creation, He created light and darkness, the sun and the moon, land and sea, and male and female of each animal. As we have seen, mercy and truth must both be in our lives in order for us to be balanced. These crucial characteristics of God complement each other. It is imperative that we not be content with being one-legged people. If you are content with having mercy but not truth or truth but not mercy, you are going to be a one-legged Christian. You will never be effective in your relationship with God nor in your relationship with people if you are content with being strong in only one of these areas. Each will not function properly without the other. A one-legged man cannot run. He may want to run, may pray to run, may wish to run, but as my dad used to say, "If wishes were fishes, we'd all have a fry!"

It is through mercy and truth together that we walk, that we run, that we move forward. A person who is one legged may say, "Well that one leg, that mercy area, is a strong leg. My muscles are so well developed there." That is a wonderful thing, but that one strong leg still does not help you run any better, because a one-legged man cannot run. With only mercy or only truth we can only hop! We need to consistently, persistently evaluate where we are and determine by the grace of God that we are going to develop both mercy and truth. Then, we need to dispense that mercy and truth consistently, persistently in every relationship we have.

In Proverbs 3:4 we are given a very strong motivation—a fourfold motivation—for maintaining the balance between mercy and truth. God says if we will bind mercy and truth around our neck and write them upon our heart, we will receive these blessings as a result. Proverbs 3:4 lists four "finds"– four discoveries that follow mercy and truth:

1. You will find favor with God.
2. You will find good understanding in the sight of God.
3. You will find favor with man.
4. You will find good understanding in the sight of man.

Notice the principle of balance at work here once again. There are two benefits that we receive in our relationship with God and two for our relationship with other people. Notice also the order—favor precedes good understanding, and our relationship with God precedes our relationship with men.

If your focus is only on getting along with people, you will never get along with people; when you make your priority getting along with God and gaining His favor and His understanding then you can properly relate to other people. If a person is committed to developing a vertical relationship that is right and proper with God, that will ultimately lead to a better ability to relate to people. This is why when you leave the God factor out of your life, your personal relationships go haywire. The relationship between God and you is the foundation for every other relationship you have. So, let's look at what you receive when you gain God's favor.

There are many men and women in the Bible of whom it was said that they had obtained favor of the Lord. The word 'favor' is used eighty-one times in your English Bible; seventy-two occasions in the Old Testament and nine in the New Testament. In the Old Testament, the word 'favor' is not always translated 'favor.' The word is also translated in the Old Testament as 'grace.' In fact, the first time this specific word is used is in Genesis 6 of a man named Noah. The Bible says, "Noah found grace in the eyes of the Lord." (Genesis 6:8) Noah made the wonderful discovery that by being a man of mercy and of truth he found grace. The Bible tells us in the New Testament that Noah was a preacher of righteousness. While he was building an ark for the salvation of his family, he was also witnessing, trying to get other people to board the ark with him. He never cut corners. He never compromised. He was a man with an impeccable commitment to truth, but he was also a man of mercy who had spent 120 years preaching to save people from the coming flood.

What does it mean to be favored of God? It simply means to be graced by God. It is God doing us a favor or God favoring you and me. There is no one whose favor you need any more than the favor of God. The one man in the Old Testament of whom this subject is talked about more than any other is Moses. In a conversation between Moses and God, we see the subject of obtaining or finding God's favor comes up. Exodus 33:12 says, *"And Moses said unto the Lord, see thou saith unto me bring up this people, and thou hast not let me know whom thou will send with me yet thou hast said I know thee by name and now has also found grace in my sight."* Moses is reminding God of what He said. I do not know when God said this to him; it might have been of the burning bush. It is no surprise that he found favor, for Moses was a man of impeccable, consistent mercy and truth.

But, I want you to notice what Moses asked for in Exodus 32:13, *"Now therefore I pray thee, if I have found grace in thy sight show me now thy way."* What Moses is asking for here is what Proverbs calls good understanding. Moses is saying, "God, if I really have been given favor from You, then I need good understanding to go along with it." Remember that a one-legged man cannot run. It is not enough to receive grace from God but not direction. Grace is the desire and the strength to commit ourselves to doing the will of God. God gave Moses that. Moses recognized that he needed more than the desire to fulfill the will of God; he also needed direction in fulfilling the will of God. That is the combination of favor and good understanding that God promises to those who keep mercy and truth.

Someone who came to see me this last week said, "I have a great desire to preach the gospel. I want to serve Jesus with my life, but I don't know what to do." This was a man who has been favored of the Lord. He has received grace, the desire to make a commitment to serving God with his life, but he properly recognized that he needs direction to go along with it. God does not just give us one principle, but he balances it with two. We have to ask for favor and good understanding, and we have to look for it. Moses talked with the Lord about it. He was at a crossroads as it were, in his leadership with the children of Israel. He had many questions: Where do we go from here? How is it all going to work out? How will we survive this journey? How do I keep the people from killing each other...or me?

Thanks be unto God that when He gives us favor, He also provides us with good understanding. Notice the next statement that Moses makes in verse 13, "that I may know thee." It is a good thing to know God's direction in our lives and to have the desire and grace to fulfill it, but ministry is more than what God is doing *through* us for others; it is also what God is doing *in* us while are ministering to others. Moses rightly recognized God's direction in his life. "God, You have highly graced me. You have favored me and given me a desire and a willingness to commit myself at eighty years of age to go back to the land where I was the most wanted criminal and lead millions of people out of Egyptian bondage having absolutely no idea how this was going to happen. Now, here we are. What are we going to do in the future? God, I need Your direction. I do not even know the way, let alone how to lead two or three million people. More than that, I need to find out more about You."

Whatever direction God has in your life and mine, wherever and whatever He has us doing for Him, it is not simply to get the job done. It is, even more importantly, to change us. Sometimes, when we evaluate our lives and our ministries, and we evaluate them simply on success in the outward sense, we become discouraged. We may say, "God, it doesn't look like I'm getting anywhere." Don't you think Moses could have said that? For forty years, they wandered in the wilderness. That process was about more than just what God was doing through the leader in leading those people; it was more importantly about what God was doing in the leader. We need to maintain the awareness that God is not only directing us but also developing us through the circumstances of life. Everyone and everything that comes into your life as you navigate through the pathway of the will of God is there for the purpose of development.

People who live only in their comfort zone in the Christian life and refuse to step out by faith and get busy serving the Lord Jesus Christ miss these lessons. Even worse, they never really get to know God. You are not going to get to know God just sitting in a classroom. You have got to roll up your sleeves and get out there on the battlefield. Then you will get to know the Master of our Salvation. I never want to lose sight of the fact that God is using me in my life as a leader to direct others, but at the same time He is developing me. As I direct, God develops. When I stop directing, God stops developing. There are people right now who are doing nothing for God. There is so much they could be doing, but they are not doing anything. That hinders the ministry of a church; but even more, it hinders the individual. You will never know God and who He is unless you are part of this process.

Then at the end of verse 13, notice that Moses said, "that I may find grace in thy sight." He has circled all the way around and is back at square one. This process is a continuing cycle. When we commit to mercy and truth, we receive favor and good understanding. As we serve Him and get to know Him better, He brings us to a place where we need more grace and more understanding. This is not a one-time process. It is something that you have to constantly be seeking after—the understanding of what God is doing both directionally and developmentally in your life. Learn it today, and you will need more tomorrow. Then, you will need more the next day. It is a marvelous process, but it also contains a grave danger.

In Numbers 11, we find the story of Moses being overwhelmed by the task. When the children of Israel left Egypt, they were happy and excited, but it did not take them long to lose the joy of their salvation and begin to murmur and complain. Day after day, month after month, year after year, Moses was leading the people in the desert because they refused to go forward with God into the Promised Land. As a result of that, Moses reached a critical point in his own life. The people complained of hunger and so God provided manna. Then, they complained because they did not have any meat to eat. They were upset with Moses, and as a result, Moses became very upset with God.

Then Moses heard the people weep throughout their families, every man in the door of his tent: and the anger of the LORD was kindled greatly; Moses also was displeased. And Moses said unto the LORD, Wherefore hast thou afflicted thy servant? and wherefore have I not found favour in thy sight, that thou layest the burden of all this people upon me? Have I conceived all this people? have I begotten them, that thou shouldest say unto me, Carry them in thy bosom, as a nursing father beareth the sucking child, unto the land which thou swarest unto their fathers? Whence should I have flesh to give unto all this people? for they weep unto me, saying, Give us flesh, that we may eat. I am not able to bear all this people alone, because it is too heavy for me. And if thou deal thus with me, kill me, I pray thee, out of hand, if I have found favour in thy sight; and let me not see my wretchedness. Numbers 11:10-15

As Moses was listening to God, Moses did okay; but when he started listening to the voices of the people, the Bible says he was displeased. The word for displeased literally means "to come apart into pieces." Moses fell apart! Notice the difference in response. God was angry because the people were sinning. Moses was discouraged and became angry at God. Moses was not thinking scripturally. He was not even thinking sanely. This happens when we get our focus off of God and start listening to the voices of those around us. Moses concluded, "God, this is Your fault." Moses even asked God to kill him. Here is the point: Moses began to doubt God's favor. When Moses became discouraged over what was happening in his ministry, he allowed himself to get displeased with God.

God allows circumstances in our lives very similar to those Moses experienced. Things do not turn out the way we plan. Don't ever get angry at God. God is too wise to make a mistake. He has never made a mistake, and He is not going to start making them with you. If we choose (in our problems) to accuse God, we are on our way to wrong thinking and wrong desires. We are on our way to personal destruction. Hold on to mercy and truth, and never doubt God's favor toward you. Hebrews 13:5 says, "Be content with such things as ye have: for he hath said, I will never leave thee nor forsake thee."

chapter 7

Teacher's Pet

My son, forget not my law; but let thine heart keep my commandments: For length of days, and long life, and peace, shall they add to thee. Let not mercy and truth forsake thee: bind them about thy neck; write them upon the table of thine heart: So shalt thou find favour and good understanding in the sight of God and man.—Proverbs 3:1-4

In school, if one particular student was favored over the others, we called them the teacher's pet. I was never the teacher's pet. In fact, everybody in my class knew who the teacher's pet was, and we all envied him. I did not understand back then why the teacher would single one child out of a classroom and give them special attention and favor. Now that I am older, I understand it a little better! And in the same way that our teacher picked out someone, God says, "Listen; out of all My children, all My students, every saved person, I favor some of My children over the others. They are My favorites." Now, some people do not like this truth. They think it is unfair for God to single out certain people. God can do whatever what God wants to do; and by definition, whatever God chooses to do is just and right.

The question then becomes, if we know that God chooses some people for His favor and blessing, who does He choose? Well, when Solomon instructs his son, it gives us insight—God favors those who do not let mercy and truth run away from them. Are you so committed to mercy that you give mercy even to those who do not deserve mercy? Are you so committed to truth that you are transparently honest, even when you might gain a temporary advantage through dishonesty? If so, then God sees that beautiful combination in your life and will favor you. Remember that this must be internalized and not simply external. "Bind them about thy neck" is external; "write them upon the tables of thine heart" is internal. If we only wear mercy and truth externally, it is hypocrisy. They must also be written upon the table of our hearts. Then, God gives the promise that we have already looked at to provide favor and good understanding with Him and with other people. Let's look at how God's favor played out in the lives of some of His "pets."

The first time the Hebrew word for favor is used is in Genesis 6:8: *"but Noah found grace* (the same word used for favor in Proverbs 3:4) *in the eyes of the Lord."* This is referring to something special that Noah received that no one else on earth had at that time. Noah found favor in God's sight. Though the world in which he lived was very wicked, and it would have been easy to write them off as deserving of the punishment that was coming, Noah still faithfully warned them of impending judgment. Noah cared about people. But, he was not just filled with mercy for them; he also cared enough about them to tell them the truth.

Noah did not earn God's grace and favor; no one does. But God has established a principle as certain as that of sowing and reaping—when we hold mercy and truth internally and externally, we will find favor and good understanding.

The Bible says that God favored Abraham. What mercy he had towards his nephew Lot! Lot did not deserve it; but nevertheless, Abraham laid his life on the line for him. He was also a man to who was committed to truth. Yes, he occasionally strayed from the truth, but he always returned to it. We could talk about Joseph. Why did God favor Joseph? It is because Joseph was a man who demonstrated consistent mercy and also consistent truth. Joseph extended such incredible mercy towards his brothers when he had the power to get revenge for their mistreatment of him. Yet, Joseph was a man who was also deeply committed to this matter of truth and honesty. We could talk about Moses. The Bible says God favored Moses. Moses had a special place in the heart of God, but Moses was another man who consistently and persistently demonstrated both mercy and truth.

We could talk about the nation of Israel. The nation of Israel, God said of them, "I have favored them. I give them special blessing and special privileges; and as long as they live and behave with mercy and with truth, I will continue to do so." We could talk about Samuel. Even as a little lad, he was so deeply favored by God that he was given great, deep understanding of the Scriptures as a result of his commitment to mercy and truth in his life. When God says, "I will give you favour and good understanding in the sight of God and man," He is not just talking in generalities. God means very specifically that He has special favors for those who keep both mercy and truth.

We could talk about Esther. She did not have to identify herself as a Jewess. She was safe in her position as the queen. She could have kept quiet and allowed all of her family to be killed. She could have protected herself, but because she was a godly woman committed to truthfulness and honesty and at the same time mercy, she spoke out to save her people, and God favored her. The Bible says God favored Job. Job recognized that even in the midst of losing his ten children to death in a single day; losing a his wealth and his camels and sheep and oxen; losing all his servants, except for three; losing his health; and even losing the love and affection of his wife. In Job 10:12 he said, "Thou hast granted me life and favour." We could talk about Mary, the only person of whom it was said "thou are highly favoured." (Luke 1:28) But, I want to focus our attention on David as the best example of the granting and effects of God's favor on someone's life.

Psalm 5:12 says, "*For thou, Lord, wilt bless the righteous with favor; thou wilt compass him about as with a shield.*" David was acknowledging that favored believers receive special protection from God. In Psalm 41, David brings this concept up again and references it happening in his life. Psalm 41:11 says, "*By this I know that thou favourest me, because mine enemy doth not triumph over me.*" David's world was a dangerous world, and David needed divine protection. Who would doubt David's mercy and David's transparent honesty? There were times when he could have taken Saul's life, yet David refraining demonstrated the absolute commitment that this man had to mercy. Most of the Psalms were written by this sweet psalmist of Israel, this poet. God gave him an enormous amount of truth that he demonstrated even when he was caught in sin. Read Psalm 51, and you will see a man confessing in honesty his wrongdoing.

No wonder David could say of God, "You have favored me." Because David was a man committed to mercy and truth, God protected him. Think about this: in his youth, David watched his father's sheep. One night, a lion came roaring and took a lamb into its mouth. Now most of us would not think, "I'm going to go kill that lion." I would have said something like, "I hope you enjoy a mutton supper tonight, Mr. Lion." But, David boldly went with incredible courage, grabbed the lion by the beard, slew the lion, and rescued the lamb. Now you may ask, "Why did David do something which seemed so humanly foolish?" I believe David knew that he lived under the divine protection of God. It may take great courage, but you can accomplish the impossible when you have the protection of God over you. Later on, David saw a bear come upon the sheep. David went after the bear, grabbed the bear, and slew it. I am not talking about hunting with a rifle; David had a slingshot and his bare hands.

The lessons David learned about God's protection while he was tending sheep were important because a few years later, David was sent by his father to take food to his brothers fighting against the Philistines. When he got there, Goliath was blaspheming God and challenging the Israelites to a man-to-man duel to the death.

David basically said, "Why doesn't somebody do something about that loud mouth?" And they looked at him and said, "Do you see how big he is?" They took David to Saul, and the king despised his youth. He did not think David was up to the task of fighting a trained warrior. David said, "Let me tell you who I am. I may be young, but I live under the divine protection of Jehovah God. I went after a lion one day, and I slew the lion. I went after a bear one day, and I slew that bear. And the same God that delivered me from them will give me the victory over Goliath!"

If you are not living in mercy and truth, you do not want to face a lion. And make no mistake about it—you do not have any choice. The lion is pacing to and fro seeking someone to devour. He is roaring after your soul. The reason he is succeeding in destroying so many Christian's lives is that we are not committed to mercy and to truth, and thus we do not receive the protection that comes with God's favor. For more than a decade, Saul tried to kill David. As far as we know, David never had an army bigger than 400 men. How many tens of thousands of soldiers did Saul have? Yet, God divinely protected David from being destroyed by Saul. Why? Because David was a man who was committed to mercy and committed to truth. He enjoyed divine protection.

The few defeats that David experienced occurred when David failed to operate by the principle of mercy and truth. When David's son Amnon raped his half-sister Tamar, David showed mercy but no truth. Amnon deserved to die for that horrible act, yet David did not punish him at all. After waiting two years, Absalom took matters into his own hands and killed Amnon. Now David showed all truth and no mercy. Absalom hid for years, and even after he was allowed to return to Jerusalem, David refused to meet with him. Most of David's children became reprobate because, in this area, rather than maintaining a balance of mercy and truth as he had with Saul, within his own family he forsook on the one hand truth or on the other hand mercy. Therefore, David suffered great sorrow in his life over his children.

Think of the example of Uriah the Hittite, one of David's mighty men—his most loyal and trusted soldiers. Was it a merciful thing for David to lay with another man's wife? No, it was a cruel, wicked thing for him to do. Was it a truthful thing? No, it was done in secret, and then it was hidden. Then, Bathsheba sent a note to the king that said, "I'm expecting a child." Uriah was a faithful soldier, a servant of the king, and he was away at war (where David should have been). David should have called Uriah home and went face-to-face with him and said, "Uriah, I had immoral relations with your wife. She's expecting my child." David should have confessed. He should have been truthful. You may have a pattern of being filled with mercy and being filled with truth as David did, but what you have done in the past is not good enough for today. There is not a person reading this who could not make the decision, "I'm going to cover that sin God instead of confess it and forsake it." Don't let mercy and truth run away!

The second benefit received when God favors someone who lives with mercy and truth is prosperity. We find this clearly outlined in Psalm 30.

Sing unto the Lord, O ye saints of his, and give thanks at the remembrance of his holiness. For his anger endureth but a moment; in his favour is life: weeping may endure for a night, but joy cometh in the morning. And in my prosperity I said, I shall never be moved. Lord, by thy favour thou hast made my mountain to stand strong: thou didst hide thy face, and I was troubled. Psalm 30:4-7

Sometimes, we are reluctant to show mercy because of the fear we will be taken advantage of by someone else. The truth is that in mercy and truth you will experience greater blessings than you ever have before. David recognized that favored believers receive special prosperity from the Lord. Psalm 30 was written for the celebration at the dedication of David's temple. David had taken Jerusalem and established it as his capital. Hiram, king of Tyre, sent down wood and stone and carpenters and skilled builders. They built David a beautiful home. It was common in Bible times for the homes of the believers to be dedicated to God. This service reminded them that their home belonged to God and was to be used for His glory. So, at the dedication of David's beautiful home where he would live, David writes that inspired Psalm. He recognizes that his prosperity was a direct result of God's favor on his life.

To find a measure of David's prosperity, look at First Chronicles 29. Here, at the end of David's life, after years of living with mercy and truth and receiving the favor of God, David began to gather materials which Solomon could use to build the Temple. To inspire the people to join him in giving, he listed his personal contributions for the project.

Moreover, because I have set my affection to the house of my God, I have of mine own proper good, of gold and silver, which I have given to the house of my God, over and above all that I have prepared for the holy house, Even three thousand talents of gold, of the gold of Ophir, and seven thousand talents of refined silver, to overlay the walls of the houses withal: The gold for things of gold, and the silver for things of silver, and for all manner of work to be made by the hands of artificers. And who then is willing to consecrate his service this day unto the Lord? 1 Chronicles 29:3-5

In today's money, that would be several hundred million dollars of gold and silver that David gave. Here was a man who was remarkably prosperous. Why? David prospered because he received God's favor. I'm not saying that if you have mercy and truth, you will be a multi-millionaire; I am saying God will make you to prosper. Do you want the favor of God in your life? Do you recognize the need of divine protection? Would you like to have His help in becoming as prosperous as God's plan is for your life? Then, here is how you do it: *"Let not mercy and truth forsake thee, bind them about thy neck, write them upon the table of thine heart; so shall thou find favor with God."* And . . . you will become the teacher's pet.

chapter 8

Learning the
Ropes

My son, forget not my law; but let thine heart keep my commandments: For length of days, and long life, and peace, shall they add to thee. Let not mercy and truth forsake thee: bind them about thy neck; write them upon the table of thine heart: So shalt thou find favour and good understanding in the sight of God and man.—Proverbs 3:1-4

We have talked about the tendency of mercy and truth to want to run away from each other—and from us. And, we have talked about the process of preventing that; how we can go about binding them about our necks (showing them externally) and writing them on our hearts (having them internally). We have talked about what the favor of God is, and what blessings it brings to our lives. Now, it is time to look at the second benefit of keeping mercy and truth—good understanding with God and man.

The Hebrew word that God selected to put right here in Proverbs 3:4 translated "good understanding" is found in the Bible sometimes translated discretion, knowledge, policy, prudence, sense, wisdom, or wise. The first time this specific word that you are looking at here in the language in which the Bible was originally written is found is in I Samuel 25. I think the story here will help grasp what it means to have good understanding. The story here is about a beautiful woman named Abigail. Even better than praising her appearance, the Bible says she was a woman of good understanding. She was married to a churlish man named Nabal. Obviously, the good understanding that she got from God happened after she got married, because she married a real dud.

When David was fleeing, trying to avoid conflict with Saul and hiding here and there around Israel, he and his soldiers needed food; so he sent his soldiers over to ask Nabal for help. Nabal treated them badly. He refused to help and sent them on their way. He didn't think anything of it because he lacked the good understanding Abigail possessed. She recognized the principle of cause and effect that had been set in motion. She understood that her husband's mistreatment of David and his servants would result in David coming with his army and wiping out her family. Nabal was clueless. He did not understand what he had done. If he had not been married to a woman with good understanding, he would have been destroyed.

Without good understanding, we make decisions without ever considering the consequences. We fulfill an immediate gratification, a desire, a lust for something we wanted to do without ever thinking about the effect of what we are doing. People who possess understanding have an insight into what happens, and they apply that to their decisions because they can see not just what is now, but also what is going to happen. That describes Abigail perfectly. She immediately got on a donkey and loaded food on other donkeys, and she set off after David's servants. She was right. When she met David and his army, David was mad. In fact, he was on his way to kill her husband and her family. She stepped in and intervened and save them because she had good understanding.

This word is used nearly 300 times in the Bible, and the concept is very important. The first time the concept of understanding comes up in our English Bible is Genesis 11 in the story of the Tower of Babel. This is the foundation of all false religion in the world even today. The people gathered to build a tower as a center of worship, but it was a works-based religion. Nothing we can do will make us acceptable to God. It is only God reaching down that saves our miserable souls from condemnation and Hell. It is not our good works; it is not our good deeds; it is not being a good neighbor or good friend that outweighs the bad. No we are all bad, and we are all deserving of Hell. Salvation is only by God's grace; it has never been by works.

So, God looked at those people building a tower up to heaven, and the Bible says, "He confounded their language." Up until that time, the whole world spoke one language, but God changed that in an instant. Why? Genesis 11:7 says, *"that they may not understand one another's speech."* There is a difference between knowing a word and knowing the meaning of the word. I came home one day and our 17-year-old daughter Jodi was listening to a group of Italian singers. Of course, they do not sing in English, they sing in Italian, but Jodi has the words of the song memorized so she can sing along. She was singing at the top of her lungs, and she knew all the words, but she doesn't know Italian. If you come up to her and use those same words in a conversation, she would not be able to answer you. She has a (limited) knowledge of Italian, but she doesn't have understanding.

One of the great dilemmas that we have in Christianity today is that too many people are content with knowing the words without understanding them. They can tell you all the Bible stories and quote all the Scriptures to you, but they have absolutely no concept of what God is talking about. Knowledge you can get on your own, but understanding you can only get from God. Simply knowing what Bible says is not enough to successfully navigate through life. The devil knows the Bible. He can quote it. He quoted Scripture to the Lord Jesus in the temptation, but does he understand it? No. And neither will we apart from God. If we could understand God, His ways, and His word apart from Him, we would have reason to be proud. God makes it clear to us that no understanding that we have in spiritual matters is innate within ourselves. We are hopelessly and helplessly ignorant, so that He gets all the honor and glory and praise.

I can remember this truth very clearly from my own life. As a teenager, I wanted to do my own thing and go my own way away from God. I was still going to church, I was the president of the youth group, I won all the prizes and everything, but my heart was not right with God. I found church to be so boring. I thought the pastor was studying how to be more boring. Then,

I got right with God on a Friday night. I walked down that aisle with thousands of people in that room that evening, and I didn't know anybody else was there. I just knew God was calling me. I went down that aisle, and I got thoroughly right with God. I did it in front of my friends; it did not matter if it was cool or not. I wanted to be like Christ. At the same time I got right with God, something happened to my preacher. The next Sunday morning when I went to church, he had improved marvelously since the last time I had heard him! However, he did not change; my understanding changed.

Proverbs 1:5 says, *"A wise man will hear and will increase learning, and a man of understanding shall attain unto wise counsel."* The phrase, "wise counsel" is actually a nautical term that carries the idea of "managing the ropes." If you have previously heard the expression "learning the ropes," this is where it comes from. When a sailor would go to sea, one of the first things they would teach him was how to tie different knots, how to raise and lower the sails, how to secure the boat to a dock. If you knew the ropes, you could do almost anything on the ship. You could take advantage of the wind to speed your progress through the water. You could navigate away from storms and dangerous reefs. A person with good understanding from God knows the ropes.

When I was about ten years old, someone gave me a scale model of a three-masted schooner to build. It was wood. I began constructing it per the instructions that came with it. I built the body of the ship and put the masts down in it, and then tried to set the sails up. The model came with a whole bunch of string for the ropes. It did not just have one little rope that went to each sail. Each sail had many ropes, and there were multiple sails. I had strings going here and strings going there. I ended up giving up. I had a model ship all right, but it was a three-masted schooner without ropes. If you are going to make it through life without shipwrecking your life, your marriage, your parent-child relationships, your business relationship, your relationship with God, your relationship with your neighbors, your brothers and sisters in Christ, and your siblings; if you hope to live life without shipwreck, God says, "You need My understanding to learn the ropes."

Solomon did not just give this advice about the importance of understanding to others; he followed it himself. When Solomon was still a teenager, he was the king of Israel. One night, God came to him at Gibeon and offered him a blank check. First Kings 3:5 says, *"In Gibeon the Lord appeared to Solomon in a dream by night, and God said ask what I shall give thee?"* What would you ask for first? What is most important to you to receive from God?

Here is Solomon's answer:

And Solomon said, thou hast showed unto thy servant David, my father great mercy according as he walked before thee in truth and in righteousness and in uprightness of heart with thee; and thou hast kept for him this great kindness that thou hast given him a son to sit on his throne as it is this day: and now O Lord, my God, thou hast made thy servant king instead of David my father, and I am a little child, I know not how to go out or come in; and thy servant is in the midst of this people, which thou hast chosen, a great people that cannot be numbered or counted for multitude. Give therefore, thy servant an understanding heart. I Kings 3:6-9

When he was presented with a blank check from God, why did Solomon ask for understanding rather something else? It is unusual for a teenager given that opportunity not to ask for cars (well, chariots anyway), power, money, long life, or many other things before understanding. The motivation for Solomon's request was the influence of his father. In verse 6, Solomon said, *"Thou hast showed unto thy servant David, my father great mercy according as he walked before thee in truth."* Is not that amazing? Mercy and truth in David's life were so obvious that his son recognized them and wanted them and the favor and understanding they produced in his own life as well. David made the importance of understanding very clear to Solomon when he was training him to take the throne. First Chronicles 22:11&12 says, *"Now my son the Lord be with thee and prosper thou, and build the house of the Lord thy God as he hath said of thee. Only the Lord give thee wisdom and understanding."*

The more we know about Solomon's training, the less surprising is his request for understanding. David specifically taught Solomon the value and importance of good understanding and modeled mercy and truth before his eyes. What have you taught your children about their priorities for life? If God came and offered them a blank check, what would they ask Him to give them? What would they say you have trained them to seek? Are they seeing mercy and truth producing understanding in your daily life? What would they say the measure of success in life is? Have you taught them the importance of learning the ropes?

Notice the reference that Solomon made to his father and

his father's relationship with God. In verse six he said, *"Now hast shown unto thy servant David, my father…"* It is striking that when Solomon thought of his dad, he did not just simply think of a great king, he thought of David as God's servant…and as a result, notice how Solomon refers to himself in his relationship with God in verse seven, *"And now, O Lord my God, thou hast made thy servant King and instead of David my father…"* Solomon wanted to have the same kind of relationship with God that his father had. This principal of emulation of our heroes is so important. If you tell me who a young person's heroes are, I can predict his future. Our children's heroes ought to be men and women who are God's servants. There is no higher or a more noble calling in life than to be the servant of God.

There is another character trait of Solomon revealed in this passage: his humility. He refers to himself in verse seven as a little child, *"I know not how to go out or come in."* Solomon was the son of the King. He was a prince. His father was a man of incredible wealth, influence, and power. Often, children of people of high success are arrogant, self-centered, whining, and egotistical. Yet Solomon, when he thought about himself as he was talking with God said, "You know God, I am just a little child. I do not know how to go my own way." That is sincere, genuine humility. Promotion and honor do not come from self; they come from God. Solomon recognized that God was the one Who had given him the privileged responsibility to be king over all Israel. Therefore, he had full confidence that he could, in humility ask God for understanding.

I think another reason Solomon was prompted to ask for understanding was because of his sense of responsibility. Notice in verse eight, he says, *"Thy servant is in the midst of thy people…"* Solomon recognized that the people he would be serving were not his. They were not there to serve him, but he was there to serve them and lead them under God. He had a sense of responsibility for God's people that led him to want to live his life in such a way that he would direct the nation to honor God. He had learned from his father David that his primary responsibility to the people was to lead them in worshipping and serving God.

I want to learn the ropes. I want to learn to navigate through this treacherous life that we live. I want to be able to navigate the ship of my life successfully, not just for myself, but for others. I have children. I have grandchildren. I have a congregation . I must set the right example for them. I take my responsibilities seriously. And, just as Solomon did, if I had the opportunity to be handed a blank check, I would say, "If I get anything from You, God, I would like to have an understanding heart." The same God Who gave understanding to Solomon will give it to you and me! We have a responsibility to live our lives in such a way in our sphere of influence that when people look at us they are going to see us as God's servants. We need to recognize that the opportunities and privileges that God has given to us are not of our own making or something that we can be proud of, but we need to in humility recognize and acknowledge it is all of Him. Then, we need to be serious about this matter of our responsibility to others. We are an influence for either good or evil to everyone we know. God has placed us strategically in this world, in this culture, in this generation, so that we can make a personal, spiritual, and eternal difference in people's lives. But, it will not take place apart from divine understanding. Learn the ropes and sail the seas successfully.

chapter 9

Removing Fear and Stress Through Mercy & Truth

And Jacob went on his way and the angels of God met him. And when Jacob saw them, he said, This is God's host: and he called the name of that place Mahanaim. And Jacob sent messengers before him to Esau his brother unto the land of Seir, the country of Edom. And he commanded them saying, Thus shall ye speak unto my lord Esau; Thy servant Jacob saith thus, I have sojourned with Laban, and stayed there until now: And I have oxen, and asses, flocks, and menservants, and womenservants: and I have sent to tell my lord, that I may find grace in thy sight. And the messengers returned to Jacob saying, We came to thy brother Esau, and also he cometh to meet thee, and four hundred men with him. Then Jacob was greatly afraid and distressed: and he divided the people that was with him, and the flocks, and herds, and the camels, into two bands; And said, If Esau come to the one company, and smite it, then the other company which is left shall escape. And Jacob said, O God of my father Abraham, and God of my father Isaac, the Lord which sadist unto me, Return unto thy country, and to thy kindred and I will deal well with thee: I am not worthy of the least of all the mercies, and of all the truth which thou hast shewed unto thy servant; for with my staff I passed over this Jordan; and now I am become two bands. Deliver me, I pray thee, from the hand of my brother, from the hand of Esau: for I fear him, lest he will come and smite me, and the mother with the children. And thou saidest, I will surely do thee good, and make thy seed as the sand of the sea, which cannot be numbered for multitude." –Genesis 32:1-12

I personally do not want my life to be a wasted effort. I have a commitment to profoundly impacting my world—the world where God has placed me, my generation, my sphere of influence—in a positive way. What I want you to see in this story from the life of Jacob is how that mercy and truth can change a person, taking away their fear and stress and giving them an opportunity at a second chance to have a positive influence on others. You know the story of Jacob and Esau, how Jacob conspired with his mother Rebekah to deceive Isaac and steal the blessing from his twin brother. Esau's heart was filled with bitterness, and he plotted his revenge. Rebekah told her favorite son, "Jacob, I want you to go to Laban's house for a few days until your brother's anger subsides." She did not understand the wounds of a bitter spirit and how that anger would never subside unless there was reconciliation between those brothers. Jacob ended up staying with Laban for twenty years, and then God instructed Jacob to go back home.

Now Jacob had received word that Esau was coming to meet him with a small army. I am sure his stress level went off the charts. There was no reason for Esau to bring 400 men to meet

Jacob unless he had bad intentions. Wisely, Jacob sent messengers to his brother saying, "Your servant Jacob is coming back to the land, and he wanted you to know." He was not even going to claim the family relationship with Esau. And, after the way he had treated Esau, it was probably a very good idea. God had promised Rebekah before her sons were born that Jacob would receive His favor. But, when Rebekah and Jacob took matters into their own hands, it ruptured the family relationship. God does not need your help to work things out. He has never and will never commission you to do something wrong to help Him out.

The night before his first meeting in twenty years with his brother, Jacob was greatly afraid and distressed and rightfully so. But notice what Jacob does and his relationship to mercy and truth. First, Jacob focused his mind on God and His mercy and truth. When Jacob was greatly afraid and distressed, he responded by making sure his focus went outward and upward rather than inward. We must recognize circumstances and situations; we must not be oblivious to danger; and we must not make that our meditation. We are not meant to be thinking of ourselves completely. People who get immersed in themselves are doomed to be people of fear and stress. Jacob changed his focus from himself to others and then to God; then he was able to be changed and to eventually reconcile with his brother.

Let's see how this process worked in Jacob's life. In the beginning, he only cared about himself. He was willing to lie to and deceive his father, steal from his brother, and do whatever it took to get what he wanted. When Jacob first heard that Esau was coming, he divided the people that were with him; the flocks and the herds and the camels. Basically, what Jacob said was, "When my brother comes with his 400 soldiers, it is inevitable that I am going to get killed. Perhaps, if I have divided half of my family over here and given them provision and the other half of my family way over there and given them provision, at least some of them will be able to escape alive. This does not sound anything like the Jacob we meet earlier. To that Jacob, only looking out for number one mattered. Here in this crisis hour, Jacob refocused.

When God has placed you in situations and circumstances which give you no wiggle room, it is not a mistake. He has brought you to that position where there is going to be a confrontation; where you are going to have to deal with something you would rather avoid, and the natural response is to be filled with fear and stress. That is not the time to begin to focus your attention and meditation on yourself. If you wallow in self pity, nobody else will pity you. You will worry yourself to ruin by focusing on yourself. The difference we see in Jacob at this moment of crisis is explained by the fact that he turned his focus outward and upward. It is imperative in our times of fear and stress, whatever the source, that we change our focus and direct it away from ourselves.

It is not productive to think too much about how we got where we are. Jacob could have mulled this around in his mind and said, "You know, this is really my mother's fault. She is the one who suggested that we deceive Dad; and now here I am twenty years later, facing my brother. I am going to die tomorrow. It is all Mom's fault." He could have said, "Oh, why did I ever come back? I know God appeared to me and said to go back home. Why did I ever listen to God? Why didn't I stay there? I was making all kinds of money with Laban. Everything was looking great and now look at me. I'm going to die tomorrow." He could have done all of that, but he would have never reconciled rightly with his brother because his focus would have been on himself. It is impossible to focus on yourself, and at the same time focus on God's mercy and on God's truth.

Fear and stress are not only inevitable in life; often they are exactly what God has planned for you. God is going to put you into situations that give you no wiggle room at times. He gave no wiggle room for Jacob. He pressed him and pressed him, and finally, after twenty years, got him to face up to this situation. God may be doing that in your life. The best advice I can give you is to stop wiggling. Stop trying to get away. Get your focus off yourself and instead focus on ministering to others. Turn your focus upward to your relationship with God. Jacob could not overcome fear with money. He could not buy a right relationship with Esau and he could not reconcile with Esau. He recognized that this was insufficient to overcome fear and stress in his life. The sooner you and I can recognize that same principle, the better off we will be.

The prayer of Jacob is not typical of the way many of us pray, particularly in times of fear and stress. Jacob does say, "Help! Look down here. My brother is coming with 400 soldiers, and he is going to wipe me off the face of the earth." But, that is where most of us would stop. Jacob had a much more mature focus than just the immediate problem. He said in verse 10, *"I am not worthy of the least of all thy mercies and of all the truth which thou has shown unto thy servant."* Instead of focusing on himself, Jacob focused on what God had done for him—the mercy and truth God had shown him over the years.

It takes a concerted effort of discipline in our thinking to stop and say, "I'm not going to think about that right now. I'm going to talk with my Father in Heaven, and I'm going to focus on how merciful and truthful God has been to me." That will not be what you will naturally want to do, but that is what you must do in your time of fear and stress. Jacob took time to recount how good God had been to him. When he left home twenty years before, the only thing he had was a staff in his hand. Now, he had a family and flocks and herds and great wealth. He recognized all of that as the blessing of God. Even though he was under pressure, Jacob said, "Oh God, You have been so good to me." Again, this represents a significant change in focus for Jacob. If you would have met him twenty years earlier, he would have said, "I'll tell you why I'm so good. I'm successful because I'm a hard worker. I'm a shrewd business man." Now, he focuses on the blessings he received, acknowledging that every one of them comes from God.

Jacob also realized that he was in the place God meant for him to be. Even though it was a tight spot, a place of stress and fear, he was where God told him to go. In verse 9, Jacob reminds God that He is the one that told him to, *"Return unto thy country, and to thy kindred and I will deal well with thee:"* He said, "The only reason I'm here is because I did what You said." If you think doing what God says is always going to bring you to a place of rest and relaxation, you have got a wrong impression. God is going to put you smack dab in the middle of a conflict or a confrontation again and again. Why? Because He is committed to you focusing on how merciful and good He is and how truthful He is, so you can commit yourself to following Proverbs 3:3 & 4. He longs to hear you say, "I'm not content with just being strong in mercy, and I'm not content with just being strong in truth" like we normally and naturally do. But instead, you will say, "I am committing myself to continuous mercy. I'm going to be good and kind and generous no matter what. At the same time, I am going to be completely truthful and honest and upright."

For Jacob, that took a time of fear and stress. In his fear and distress, Jacob focused on others, and then he focused on God (specifically God's mercy and God's truth), but that is not where he stopped. Jacob also followed God's example of giving him mercy and truth by giving mercy and truth to his brother, Esau. Understand that the word for mercy is also translated generosity, goodness, or kindness in the Bible. And so, Jacob prepared a gift for Esau.

And he lodged there that same night; and took of that which came to his hand a present for Esau his brother; Two hundred she goats, and twenty he goats, two hundred ewes, and twenty rams, Thirty milch camels with their colts, forty kine and ten bulls, twenty she asses, and ten foals. Genesis 32:13-15

Jacob had never been known for his benevolence and his generosity.

But, as we have seen throughout this chapter, the Jacob of Genesis 32 and 33 is a changed man. Jacob said, "If I'm going to reconcile with Esau; If I'm going to gain favor and understanding from the brother that I wounded so unfairly and so deeply, then I'm going to have to be generous. I'm going to have to give him mercy. I'm going to be kind unto him." He sent Esau a whopping offering. If you doubt that was his motive, look in Genesis 33:8. Jacob and Esau are talking. Esau asks Jacob a question, *"And he said, What meanest thou by all this drove which I met? And he said, These are to find grace in the sight of my lord."* Do you see that? Do you understand the meaning of mercy and truth? When you and I are just good and kind and benevolent to people, and then we follow it up with transparent honesty, then that tends to give us favor and good understanding in their sight.

Jacob was humble in his approach to Esau. Genesis 33:3 says, *"And he* (Jacob) *passed over before them* (all of his family), *and bowed himself to the ground seven times, until he came near to his brother."* The expression "bowed himself to the ground" literally means that Jacob put his face in the dirt. Here is Jacob walking toward his brother who is standing off in the distance. Jacob falls flat on his face in front of his brother. He stands up and goes a few feet closer to his brother, and he falls down again, face down on the ground, gets up and takes a few more steps, and does it again. He does this seven times until he is standing nose to nose with his brother. The last words Jacob heard from Esau twenty years before were, "I'm going to kill my brother." Jacob was giving honor to his brother Esau. He was expressing, as the younger son, the authority and respect that the eldest son of a Jewish family would rightfully receive from the younger siblings in the family. Jacob was being transparently honest with his brother Esau.

God used mercy and truth to bring reconciliation between Jacob and Esau. Genesis 33:4 says, *"And Esau ran to meet him, and embraced him and fell on his neck, and kissed him: and they wept."* How fast do you think Jacob's heart was beating when he saw Esau headed toward him at a run? However, Esau was not coming to kill Jacob, he was responding to the mercy and truth he was receiving. He was coming to be reconciled to his brother.

Is an irreconcilable relationship causing you stress today? Is it causing you fear? Do you see the importance of mercy and truth to healing that relationship? First, recognize that God is merciful and truthful to you. Learn to appreciate and rejoice in that. Then, learn to follow the example of God. Reconciliation can occur if we will go out and give mercy and give truth to those with whom we need to be reconciled. When you understand that everything you have belongs to God and is a result of His goodness, you do not have to hold onto it any longer. You can give it away. When you recognize that you can have all the wealth in the world and still you are going to face fear and stress, you do not have to hang onto it. God can bring you to a place where you are willing to be generous and kind to others. What were the circumstances that led up to this reconciliation and the removal of fear and stress in Jacob's life? It only came as God Himself forced Jacob to face his sin and deal with it. If you have wounded someone, God is going to bring you to a place where you are going to have to deal with it.

The only way to deal with it is through mercy and truth, and the only way to get mercy and truth is to focus on others and then on God and His mercy and truth rather than focusing on yourself. Then, commit yourself to following His example and give mercy and truth to others. The results will be amazing!

chapter 10

When Sin Has Separated Us from God, We Need Mercy & Truth

My son, forget not my law; but let thine heart keep my commandments: For length of days, and long life, and peace, shall they add to thee. Let not mercy and truth forsake thee: bind them about thy neck; write them upon the table of thine heart: So shalt thou find favour and good understanding in the sight of God and man. —Proverbs 3:1-4

A s we have looked at the balance between mercy and truth, I have told you that these two attributes are characteristics of God Himself. They are perfectly balanced aspects of His nature. We struggle with that balance. Chances are, if you find your heart tender and forgiving, kind and generous, and good to others, even when they don't deserve your goodness, kindness, and forgiveness, that you also find it extremely difficult to tell the truth knowing how the truth can hurt. On the other hand, if you find it gratifying and exhilarating, it's quite simple for you to identify when someone has gone wrong and to identify the truth that they need to hear and give it to them, chances are you find it difficult when people disappoint you and they do not do what's right consistently and continually, to find mercy in your heart for them. Mercy and truth do not really get along very well in the same house, but God says that it is imperative that we not let mercy or truth forsake us. To help us see what this balance looks like in action, let's look at a story from the life of Moses and see how God reacts to His people with both mercy and truth.

And the Lord descended in the cloud, and stood with him there, and proclaimed the name of the Lord. And the Lord passed by before him, and proclaimed, The Lord, The Lord God, merciful and gracious, longsuffering, and abundant in goodness and truth, Keeping mercy for thousands, forgiving iniquity and transgression and sin, and that will by no means clear the guilty; visiting the iniquity of the fathers upon the children, and upon the children's children, unto the third and to the fourth generation. Exodus 34:5-7

This revelation from God that He gave directly to Moses of His being filled with mercy and at the same time filled with truth came at a very critical time in the life of Moses as well as Israel. Understanding the circumstances will give us a better understanding of the times in our lives that it is peculiarly and particularly imperative that we focus our attention on God and His great mercy and truth. There are many, many things that could be said about God. Since He is infinite, the list literally goes on forever. However, in talking about Himself and revealing Himself to Moses, God chose certain characteristics to focus on and highlight. He said, "Moses, at this time in your life and in the life of the children of Israel, it is very important for you to know that I am a God of incredible mercy and goodness and grace. I want you to know that at the same time I am a God of absolute truth and I will hold people accountable for what they do, but I will also forgive iniquity and transgressions. I'll do this again and again, because it is part of My nature and character that I am a God of mercy and truth."

What was it about the circumstances that were taking place at that time that made it essential or necessary for Moses and subsequently the people of Israel to be reminded that He is a God filled with mercy and truth? After leaving Egypt, the children of Israel made the trip to Mt. Sinai in the wilderness. There, they would receive the law of God that would dictate and govern how they were to live. Moses left the children of Israel in their camp and went up on the mountain where he received a personal revelation from God. Exodus 24:18 says, *"And Moses went into the midst of the cloud, and gat him up into the mount: and Moses was in the mount forty days and forty nights."* Exodus chapters 25 to 34 detail the time that Moses had with God on the mountain. What an incredible spiritual experience this was for Moses in the very presence of God. God spoke to Moses in a way that He did not speak to other people. The Bible says that God spoke to Moses face to face as a man speaks to a man. Moses was not aware of this; but when he came down from the mountain, because of forty days in the absolute pure presence of almighty God, his face had gained a glow like the brightness of the sun in midday. The people of Israel were afraid to even look at his countenance because the glow of God was on his face. That is an incredible spiritual experience.

Moses was there with God; and in that incredible experience, He gave to Moses the Law and the regulations, how life is to be regulated and ruled. Here, these millions of slaves who had spent nearly 400 years in Egypt as slaves to Pharaohs had now been made free. They had come across the Red Sea and the desert land, and now Moses was on the mountain receiving the law of God. Also as part of this incredible experience, while he was there on the mountain, Moses was given the description of the Tabernacle. This marvelous place of worship where God, shining in glory, would come down and where Moses, Aaron, and the seventy elders of Israel could go in before the Lord and speak with the Lord; where they could there make reconciliation between the people and God and build a place of worship. God used Moses on that mountain to describe the kind of relationship that He wanted to have with us. By the way, God spent one chapter on the rules (the law) and He spent the rest of the book on "here's how you worship Me." That's a great priority to keep in mind. Christianity is not about the rules, the regulations, or the law; it is about worshipping a thrice holy God. When you are worshipping God, in tune with Him, and in a right relationship with Him, the rules and regulations of the Christian life will not be odious to you.

I remember when I left southwestern Michigan in the fall of 1971 and drove my old Buick LeSabre to Watertown, Wisconsin, and enrolled into the "penitentiary" called Maranatha Baptist Bible College. At least I thought it was the penitentiary. I met this tall, bald-headed fellow there who was the commandant. He ran that place with an iron fist. He told us when to get up, when to go to bed, and he had the audacity to tell me, "Son, go cut your hair!" I had not been away from home ten days, and I already had somebody like my dad telling me, "Son, go cut your hair." I thought to myself, "I'm paying money to get this?" I remember I had some bell-bottomed trousers; now this is 1971, and I dared to wear them on campus on a Saturday morning. I was walking on campus when up came Dr. Cedarholm. "Son, what have you got on there?" I said, "Pants, sir." He said, "Yeah, but what are those things around the bottom?" I said, "They call them bell bottoms." He said, "They're not allowed here. Go change those clothes right now." I can remember how that irritated the fire out of me. I thought, "How did he dare? I spent good money going out and buying these pants. I think I look pretty cool in them." Back then, I had about a 32 inch waist and those bells were about 32 inches on each leg. I was styling with those pants, but that was the last time I wore them on campus.

I did not like it there. My sister, Barbara, was also there. She is four years older than me, and I did not like her either. I did not like her from the earliest day I can remember. If you have an older sister, you understand. If you do, I can guarantee you that she thought she was your second mom. That is what they all think; they think that they are the boss, and so I had two moms. I had my real mom, and then I had Barbara. Barbara bossed me. I can remember the day I was sitting in the auditorium of Berean Baptist Church and there had just been a meeting with the pastor of our church. I was there, not because I wanted to be there but because my dad said, "Son, we're going to go figure out where you are going to go to college." So we went in and talked to the preacher, then the preacher sent me out and talked to my dad for a while. Then, they called me back in and said, "Well we believe it is God's will that you go to Maranatha." I thought, Barbara's there, Dr. Cedarholm's there, and the rules are all there. I was looking for freedom. I was not looking to go to a place like that, so I can tell you I was not a happy camper when I got there.

But, something happened after I was there for a while. I grew to like that older, tall, bald-headed gentleman. I grew to love Dr. Myron Cedarholm. He was the real deal. He did not have a hypocritical bone in his body, and he had a genuine sincere love for the students. He sacrificed his life for us, and he loved us. He was strict, straight, and he was a wonderful balance of mercy and truth. When I fell in love with the president of the college and grew to appreciate him, nobody ever had to tell me to get a haircut again. I read the rules before I bought clothes, and I did not have any trouble having my music checked. Why? It was because I had a right relationship with the boss. That is why God said, "Moses, here are the commandments," but then He spent most of the rest of their forty days together talking about worship. The right relationship with the boss makes the rules easy to follow. Now, this experience was a spiritual high for Moses. But, in the camp of the Israelites, things were not going so well.

When the people saw that Moses delayed to come down out of the mount the people gathered themselves together unto Aaron, and said

unto him, Up, make for us gods, which shall go before us; for as for
this Moses, the man that brought us up out of the land of Egypt, we
wot not what is become of him. And Aaron said unto them, Break
off the golden earrings, which are in the ears of your wives, or your
sons, and of your daughters, and bring them unto me. And all the
people brake off the golden earrings which were in their ears, and
brought them unto Aaron. And he received them at their hand, and
fashioned it with a graving tool, after he had made it a molten calf:
and the said, These be thy gods, O Israel, which brought thee up out of
the land of Egypt. And they rose up early on the morrow, and offered
burnt offerings, and brought peace offerings; and the people sat down
to eat and to drink, and rose up to play." Exodus 32:1-6

God did not tell Moses how long their visit on the mountain
would last. After forty days passed, the people grew restless. They
did not know if Moses would come back or not, and so they went
to Aaron. Moses left Aaron in charge in his absence, but Aaron was
an inferior spiritual leader. There are a whole lot of men and women
today who are in spiritual leadership who are grossly inferior. It
does not take very long for a good thing to turn bad when you
have bad leadership. These children of Israel were like new young
believers. You can draw a clear analogy with their salvation being
the Passover, their baptism being walking through the Red Sea
with the water on each side and the cloud above, and now they are
making a journey to the Promised Land. But, new believers need
a solid foundation and solid leadership, or they will find it easy to
go back to their old ways. That is what the people did.

They asked Aaron to make them a god they could see to

worship. Sadly, he gave in to their demands instead of focusing their attention on the Lord. Bad leadership produces bad results in the lives of new converts. As the people began to worship the golden calf that Aaron made, the Bible says they "rose up to play." This is not talking about sporting events or entertainment; it is talking about immorality. False worship is always going to lead to immoral behavior. In fact, the Bible says later on that Aaron told them, "Hey listen, take off your clothes and dance." What kind of a leader is that? While Moses was in the midst of an incredible spiritual experience on top of the mountain, the people into whom he had poured his life were turning their backs on God. Think about all that Moses had gone through when he answered the call from a burning bush to go back into the land of Egypt at eighty years of age to bring these people out of captivity. Now, here they are less than two months into their freedom, and they have already defiled themselves. They were dancing, and they were naked, and they were living immoral lives.

It was at this moment that God declared Himself to Moses to be a God Who is both full of mercy and full of truth. Did the children of Israel need mercy in their sinful state? Of course. If not for God's mercy, they would rightly have been destroyed. But, did they also need truth? Yes. They needed to be instructed to destroy their idol, put on their clothes, and live righteously. So, Moses returned to the camp to set things right. When he came down and saw what was going on, Moses became very, very angry. In fact, he was so irritated that he took the stone tablets that he had just spent forty days on the mountain with God getting, and he broke them in front of the people. Moses was not the only one who was angry. God said to him, "Let's remove those who have sinned against Me." Exodus 32: 27 & 28 says, *"And he said unto them, Thus saith the Lord God of Israel, Put every man his sword by his side, and go in and out from gate to gate throughout the camp, and slay every man his brother, and every man his companion, and every man his neighbor. And the children of Levi did according to the word of Moses: and there fell of the people that day about three thousand men."*

You say, "Where is the mercy?" If not for mercy, God would have struck everyone in the camp dead for their sin. God shows mercy far beyond our imagining. If you think about it, when do you need to know that God is a God that is filled with mercy? When do you need to know that there is a God in heaven that is filled with truth? It is when our sin has separated us from fellowship with Him and has caused Him to become angry. Understanding God's mercy and truth should drive us back into His arms in repentance, seeking His mercy, and following His truth.

chapter 11

Mercy, Truth, Forbearance

[To the chief Musician, Altaschith, Michtam of David, when he fled from Saul in the cave.] Be merciful unto me, O God, be merciful unto me: for my soul trusteth in thee: yea, in the shadow of thy wings will I make my refuge, until these calamities be overpast. I will cry unto God most high; unto God that performeth all things for me. He shall send from heaven, and save me from the reproach of him that would swallow me up. Selah. God shall send forth his mercy and his truth. My soul is among lions: and I lie even among them that are set on fire, even the sons of men, whose teeth are spears and arrows, and their tongue a sharp sword. Be thou exalted, O God, above the heavens; let thy glory be above all the earth. They have prepared a net for my steps; my soul is bowed down: they have digged a pit before me, into the midst whereof they are fallen themselves. Selah. My heart is fixed, O God, my heart is fixed: I will sing and give praise. Awake up, my glory; awake, psaltery and harp: I myself will awake early. I will praise thee, O Lord, among the people: I will sing unto thee among the nations. For thy mercy is great unto the heavens, and thy truth unto the clouds. Be thou exalted, O God, above the heavens: let thy glory be above all the earth.—Psalm 57:1-11

As you read the Psalms, you will notice that a few of them have introductions at the beginning. These give us the details or circumstances surrounding their writing, and they are inspired by God just as the text is. Psalm 57 begins with two notations: Altashith, which means do not destroy, and Mictham, which means Golden Psalm. (There are only six Psalms so designated.)

Then, we are told that this Psalm was written by David when he fled from Saul in the cave. Twice in the Psalm, David rejoices in God's mercy and God's truth. Because we know so much about the background of the writing of this particular Psalm, this gives us a rare opportunity for us to see into the heart and particularly the mind of the writer. Why would David focus on mercy and truth at a time when he was running for his life? To understand that, let's look at story of when this Psalm was written, which is found in First Samuel 24.

And it came to pass, when Saul was returned from following the Philistines, that it was told him, saying, Behold, David is in the wilderness of Engedi. Then Saul took three thousand chosen men out of all Israel, and went to seek David and his men upon the rocks of the wild goats. And he came to the sheepcotes by the way, where was a cave; and Saul went in to cover his feet: and David and his men remained in the sides of the cave. And the men of David said unto him, Behold the day of which the LORD said unto thee, Behold, I will deliver thine enemy into thine hand, that thou mayest do to him as it shall seem good unto thee. Then David arose, and cut off the skirt of Saul's robe privily. And it came to pass afterward, that David's heart smote him, because he had cut off Saul's skirt. And he said unto his men, The Lord forbid that I should do this thing unto my master, the Lord's anointed, to stretch forth mine hand against him, seeing he is the anointed of the Lord. So, David stayed his servants with these words, and suffered them not to rise against Saul. But Saul rose up out of the cave, and went on his way. 1 Samuel 24:1-7

David was hiding from Saul in the most difficult terrain he could find. Yet, Saul and his army continued to pursue him. David was hiding with his men in a deep, dark cave when Saul walked into that very cave to take a nap. For more than decade, Saul has been trying to kill David. He has tried time and again to destroy the young man God had chosen to replace him. Now, he is sleeping apart from his army while surrounded by people who have every reason to kill him.

David's men immediately recognized the opportunity. They knew that if Saul were to die, David could ascend the throne. He had already been anointed to become king over Israel. They viewed this as God's way of making that happen. David did not. He refused to allow them to kill Saul. He did cut a piece off Saul's robe, but he felt bad for even doing that much. The Bible says his "heart smote him."

David was not willing to kill Saul because Saul was in authority. It is never right to rebel. David understood that principle, and he was willing to suffer the consequences in his own life; the agony of having to continually avoid Saul, living within the danger of being killed by Saul. Despite all that, David refused to violate the principle. David placed his trust in God instead of taking matters into his own hands. He was giving forbearance to Saul. Not only was Saul in authority, but David remembered he was the Lord's anointed. There was a spiritual reason for not attacking Saul. So, David allowed Saul to walk out of the cave alive and unharmed.

Afterward Saul rose up out of the cave and went on his way. David also arose afterward, and went out of the cave, and cried after Saul, saying, My lord the king. And when Saul looked behind him, David stooped with his face to the earth, and bowed himself. And David said to Saul, Wherefore hearest thou men's words, saying, Behold, David seeketh thy hurt? Behold, this day thine eyes have seen how that the Lord had delivered thee to-day into mine hand in the cave; and some bade me kill thee: but mine eye spared thee; and I said, I will not put forth mine hand against my lord; for he is the Lord's anointed. Moreover, my father, see, yea, see the skirt of thy robe in my hand: for in that I cut off the skirt of thy robe, and killed thee not, know thou and see that there is neither evil nor transgression in mine hand, and I have not sinned against thee; yet thou huntest my soul to take it. The Lord judge between me and thee, and the Lord avenge me of thee: but mine hand shall not be upon thee. As saith the proverb of the ancients, Wickedness proceedeth from the wicked; but mine hand shall not be upon thee. After whom is the king of Israel come out? After whom dost thou pursue? after a dead dog, after a flea. The Lord therefore be judge, and judge between me and thee, and see, and plead my cause, and deliver me out of thine hand. And it came to pass, when David had made an end of speaking these words unto Saul, that Saul said, Is this thy voice, my son David? And Saul lifted up his voice, and wept." 1 Samuel 24:8-16

This is the setting for Psalm 57. In looking at these two passages of Scripture together, we see mercy and truth together in action producing forbearance. Just as God puts up with our faults and frailties and failures, we are to do the same in our interactions with people. You do not always have to get your way. You do not always have to give retribution. You do not always have to "get a word in". Good, wholesome, healthy, lifelong relationships, both with God and others, demand forbearance; but we can only be forbearing people through the mercy and truth of God. Recently, I met a former church member in a store. He asked to talk to me, and I knew immediately what he wanted to talk about. Through a series of horrible events years before, he had been hurt very deeply. He had been counseled to offer his spouse mercy and forgiveness and remain in his marriage, but he had not. I do not think I will ever forget the look on his face as he said to me, "I'm so sorry that I didn't take that advice." He proceeded to tell me how after marriage had dissolved, the children were divided. Now, there are grandchildren being impacted by it. It has been twenty years, and not one member of that family is living for God and serving Him. Why? Because there was no mercy and truth.

It was because David was focused on God's mercy and God's truth in his life that he was able to give mercy and truth to undeserving Saul. When you are in a position that offers you the chance to get even, the tendency is for you to ruminate on how offensive that person has been to you. Your mind will try to talk you into taking vengeance, even though you know in your heart the Bible says, *"Vengeance is mine, saith the Lord, I will repay."*

(Romans 12:19) It is likely that there will be people around you saying, "God brought this position for you to bring vengeance. You have every right to do this." David had all that. He could easily have rationalized and justified killing Saul; instead, he focused on God's mercy and truth and did what was right.

I do not think it is a coincidence that Psalm 57 starts with David pleading with God for more mercy. I have discovered this truth over the years. When we give mercy to those who particularly do not deserve mercy, we need to get mercy to replace the mercy that we have given away. David had given great mercy to Saul, and he knew that the only place to find more mercy was back at the feet of the all-merciful God. Instead of demanding retribution, rather than giving them what they deserve, rather than seeking revenge, give them mercy, and then run to God for more mercy. That is what David did. He extended mercy to Saul and enlisted mercy from God. David was able to give forbearance to Saul because he knew there was a place he could turn for more mercy.

David understood natural law; that whatsoever a man soweth, that shall he also reap. If you want to receive mercy from God, you had better be giving mercy to others. Do not expect to sow judgment and retribution and get even and then expect to reap a crop of mercy from God. It does not work that way. David's confidence that God would give him mercy and truth was based on David's awareness that God operates by principle. The man that I told you about earlier has reaped a crop that has given him great sorrow. In the midst of a crowd of people at the store, I watched that grown man with tears coming down his cheeks as he poured his heart out to me. He said, "I wish I could back up. I wish I could do it again." You can't. What you can do is start sowing the right seeds today. I cannot tell you that you are not going to have a crop from what you have been sowing, but I can tell you this: you can start planting new seeds. That is what David is teaching us. Though Saul deserved to die, David said, "I'm not going to do it." He exercised forbearance, and he gave Saul mercy and truth fully expecting that he could come back to God and receive more mercy and truth.

I want to drive this point home to you—you have a responsibility to do right no matter what another person does or fails to do. If you turn over just two chapters in First Samuel, you will find David being chased by Saul again! In First Samuel 26, David has another opportunity to get even with Saul.

And David arose, and came to the place where Saul had pitched: and David beheld the place where Saul lay, and Abner the son of Ner, the captain of his host: and Saul lay in the trench, and the people pitched round about him. Then answered David and said to Ahimelech the Hittite, and to Abishai the son of Zeruiah, brother to Joab, saying, Who will go down with me to Saul to the camp? And Abishai said, I will go down with thee. So David and Abishai came to the people by night: and, behold, Saul lay sleeping within the trench, and his spear stuck in the ground at his bolster: but Abner and the people lay round about him. Then said Abishai to David, God hath delivered thine enemy into thine hand this day: now therefore let me smite him, I pray thee, with the spear even to the earth at once, and I will not smite him the second time. And David said to

Abishai, Destroy him not: for who can stretch forth his hand against the Lord's anointed, and be guiltless? David said furthermore, As the Lord liveth, the Lord shall smite him; or his day shall come to die; or he shall descend into battle, and perish. The Lord forbid that I should stretch forth mine hand against the Lord's anointed: but, I pray thee, take thou now the spear that is at his bolster, and the cruse of water, and let us go. So David took the spear and the cruse of water from Saul's bolster; and they gat them away, and no man saw it, nor knew it, neither awaked: for they were all asleep; because a deep sleep from the Lord was fallen upon them.

Then David went over to the other side, and stood on the top of an hill afar off; a great space being between them: And David cried to the people, and to Abner the son of Ner, saying, Answerest thou not, Abner? Then Abner answered and said, Who art thou that criest to the king? And David said to Abner, Art not thou a valiant man? and who is like to thee in Israel? wherefore then hast thou not kept thy lord the king? for there came one of the people in to destroy the king thy lord. This thing is not good that thou hast done. As the Lord liveth, ye are worthy to die, because ye have not kept your master, the Lord's anointed. And now see where the king's spear is, and the cruse of water that was at his bolster. 1 Samuel 26:5-16

I wish I could tell you that if you give people mercy and truth, they will respond correctly and never mistreat you again. But, it does not work that way. Even though Saul had received mercy and truth from David, just a little while later he was back trying to kill David again. Again, David has the opportunity to take revenge and kill his enemy. David went into the camp and took

Saul's canteen and Saul's spear, but he didn't take Saul's life. David gave Saul more mercy and truth. You have to admire David. How many times are we willing to exercise mercy and truth toward someone who deserves vengeance? David was a man who believed in forbearance. Even at the risk of his own life, he offered Saul mercy again and again. Sometimes, we give people mercy once or twice; but after that, we decide to cut them off. There is a reason the Bible says God's mercies are new every morning (Lamentations 3:23)—we need new mercy every day. We do not just give people mercy once. We do not give them what they have coming. We forbear. And we receive new mercy from God, so that we can keep giving mercy to others.

Because David was meditating on the certainty of God's mercy and truth, he was prepared to give it to others. Read Psalm 57 again and notice how he describes God's mercy and truth. He says they are so great that they stretch up into the sky beyond the clouds. If we reflect on how great God's mercy is to us, it is easier for us to extend that mercy to others. When you are tempted to give judgment and vengeance, read Psalm 57. Pray as David did. Say, "God, I've used up the mercy and given out the truth, and so I need some more." This is the only way you will be able to consistently keep on giving mercy and truth to people who do not deserve it.

chapter 12

Better Than Tide

By mercy and truth iniquity is purged; and by the fear of the Lord men depart from evil. –Proverbs 16:6

Mercy and truth produce amazing results as we have already seen. Now we are going to look at another facet of this wonderful pair; the power to purge us from our sins. I have no doubt that everybody has a sin problem. We may have tried to get rid of our sin on our own, but it is impossible apart from the mercy of God and the truth of God that we could ever give up that sin which doth so easily beset us. When the Bible talks about purging, the word means "to clean out, or to remove, or to take away." If you are old enough, you probably remember the Fuller Brush man. A fuller was a man or woman who washed clothes for a living. The process of cleaning clothes was called purging. The bottom line of purging was the removal of the dirt. What the Bible is saying here is that mercy and truth together is like a fantastic detergent. It removes the dirt out of our lives and makes us clean and white in our garments for God.

When Solomon was inspired to write this verse of Scripture, I wonder if he thought of his father. In his confession in Psalm 51, David talked about God's mercy and truth and about being purged from his sins. In 1946, Proctor and Gamble introduced a new laundry detergent. They had perfected a combination of ingredients that would get almost any stain out of clothing. Within three months, Tide was outselling every other brand on the market, and today it remains the best-selling laundry product in the world. But, the best laundry detergent in the world cannot remove the stain of sin. It takes the blood of the Lord Jesus Christ, God's Son. That is the process David describes in Psalm 51.

Have mercy upon me, O God, according to thy lovingkindness: according unto the multitude of they tender mercies blot out my transgressions. Wash me thoroughly from mine iniquity, and cleanse me from my sin. Purge me with hyssop, and I shall be clean; wash me, and I shall be whiter than snow. Psalm 51:1, 2 & 7

If you have iniquity in your heart–unconfessed sin before God–then God sees you as dirty. Your life is sullied by the sin. How can it be purged from your iniquity? The Bible says that purging from iniquity comes through the blood, but it comes as God dispenses it in mercy and in truth. The idea of purging appears again in Isaiah 1:25 where God says, *"And I will turn my hand upon thee, and purely purge away thy dross, and take away all thy tin:"* Purging was not only used by the person who did the laundry; it was referred to as a process used by refiners as well. Malachi 3:3 says, *"And he shall sit as a refiner and purifier of silver: and he shall purify the sons of Levi, and purge them as gold and silver, that they may offer unto the Lord an offering in righteousness."* When the Bible talks about purging something that is unnecessary or something that is impure out of our lives, it illustrates it with the process by which gold, silver, and other precious metals are purified. Ore, dug out of the earth, has impurities and less valuable metals mingling with the gold or silver. That must be removed before it is valuable and useful. Because God is filled with mercy and truth, He places us in the crucible of affliction and turns the heat up on our lives.

When God turns up the heat on your life and puts you under pressure, the dross comes to the surface. Have you responded to something and been surprised by what you said or did? Put in the right situation, you will say things that you never though you would say. Where does that come from? It comes from the inside heart of man having been brought to the surface by pressure. We tend to think that if God loved us, He would not allow us to experience so much pressure; but in reality, God's love is why He puts us in those situations. God, in His mercy and in His truth, is so committed to seeing us be pure and clean and white that He brings the pressure. God wants to bring the dross to the surface so that we will deal with it and remove it from our life.

We see the concept of purging again in an agricultural setting. Matthew 3:12 says, *"Whose fan is in his hand, and he will thoroughly purge his floor, and gather his wheat into the garner; but he will burn up the chaff with unquenchable fire."* Wheat is a wonderful and useful grain, but it comes encased in chaff which is completely worthless. The process of purging the wheat removes that which is unnecessary and unproductive so that only the good remains. In Bible times, wheat was threshed—literally beaten with sticks to knock the chaff loose. I am sure that if a grain of wheat could talk, it would have said something like, "Whoa! I don't like this winnowing. It hurts when those sticks hit me. Somebody make this stop!" Purging is the result of God's mercy and truth. I am convinced that much of our praying is spent asking God to take away things He has sent into our lives to make us more like His Son. The next time you endure painful circumstances or difficult situations, instead of trying to get out, look for something God is trying to purge from your life to make you more valuable and useful to Him.

Purging was also part of the work in the vineyard. In John 15:2 Jesus said, *"Every branch in me that beareth not fruit he taketh away: and every branch that beareth fruit, he purgeth it, that I may bring forth more fruit."* The husbandman would take the weak branches and shoots and cut them off so that the vine would produce more plentiful, plumper and juicier grapes. God looks at our lives, and He says, "You need to be pruned now and then." If you want to produce fruit for God then you must submit to His purging. It is through the purging that we produce better fruit. Have you ever seen a picture of a world record tomato or pumpkin or watermelon? Those things are huge. But they are not produced by accident. The grower takes away all the weak branches and fruit first so that what remains will be larger and stronger.

Paul described purging for Timothy as being part of the process by which we are prepared to bring honor and glory to

God. Second Timothy 2:20&21 says, *"But in a great house there are not only vessels of gold and of silver, but also of wood and of earth; and some to honour, and some to dishonour. If a man therefore purge himself from these, he shall be a vessel unto honour, sanctified, and meet for the master's use, and prepared unto every good work."* If you pull a drinking glass out of the cupboard at home and you look inside to see a big, dead spider before you put it under the tap for water, would you drink out of it anyway? No, you would wash the glass. Maybe even twice! Paul described special vessels that God had prepared for His service. But the point he was making was that it is not enough just to look good on the outside; we must be clean on the inside as well to be an honorable vessel. It is easy to put on a show and dress up for church so that everyone thinks we are doing fine, but God sees the heart. He knows when our vessels need purging, and His mercy and truth see to it that we have the opportunity to remove the evil from our lives.

Paul knew how that process worked firsthand. He had experienced it in his own life. He said of himself in I Timothy 1:13, "I was before a blasphemer, injurious, a persecutor, but I obtained mercy." You know the story how on the road to Damascus, Paul had a life-changing encounter with God. God knocked Paul to the ground, and He blinded him. You say, "Oh that's cruel." No, that's merciful, because God wanted to save his wretched soul and needed to get Paul's attention first. So, God in his mercy gave him the truth, *"Saul, Saul why persecutest thou me?"* Saul asked two questions. "Who are you?" The answer came, "I am Jesus who you are persecuting." His very next question was, "What would you have me to do?" Paul came out of that Damascus experience a different person. Before he was a persecutor and a blasphemer, but now he was a believer. God saves us by mercy and truth.

Mercy and truth purge our iniquity not only in salvation, but in our spiritual growth and development as well. We see this in the life of David when he was confronted by Nathan for his sin. God gave David mercy and truth. When Nathan confronted David, he said, "Thou art the man," but he also said, "Thou shalt not die." God balances mercy and truth in order that He might motivate us to be purged from our iniquity. And, if that is how God works with us, we also should exercise mercy and truth in our efforts to stimulate and motivate people to be purged from their iniquity. I think everyone who is reading this knows someone who has iniquity in his life that needs to be purged. How can you to help them? You are going to help them by mercy and truth, by mercy and truth, by mercy and truth, applied again and again and again, just the same way God helps us.

That is not the end of the sentence though. Proverbs 16:6 does not end with the statement about being purged. It also says, "By the fear of the Lord men depart from evil." The only acceptable response to God's mercy and God's truth is to fall on your face in fear of the Lord. When you follow your faith in the fear of the Lord, you *will* depart from evil. The balance of both mercy and truth is necessary to teach the fear of the Lord. Mercy is not enough. When we financially support someone who is living in blatant rebellion to God, we are an enabler. That is not real mercy—they desperately need the truth too. We ought never to fund someone's sin; because in so, doing we are circumventing the chastening hand of God in their lives. We hinder the chances of them fearing the Lord and departing from their iniquity.

What happens when we do not respond to mercy and truth by purging sin from our lives? We see the sad answer in the history of the children of Israel. The prophet Ezekiel described God's dealings with His people in Ezekiel 24.

She hath wearied herself with lies, and her great sum went not forth out of her: her scum shall be in the fire. In thy filthiness is lewdness: because I have purged thee, and thou wast not purged, thou shalt not be purged from thy filthiness any more, till I have caused my fury to rest upon thee. I the Lord have spoken it: it shall come to pass, and I will do it; I will not go back, neither will I spare, neither will I repent; according to thy ways, and according to thy doings, shall they judge thee, saith the Lord God. Ezekiel 24:12-14

God, in his mercy, fed the Israelites. He kept them as the apple of His eye. He blessed them in innumerable ways generation after generation. He gave them His truth through faithful men of God who proclaimed, "Thus saith the Lord." Yet, they refused to listen to His voice. That is why the prophet Ezekiel is talking to people who live, not in Israel but in Babylon. They were taken away from their land into captivity because God's mercy and truth did not lead them to purge sin from their lives. God gave them many opportunities to repent, but they refused to heed the warnings. They knew what they were supposed to do. Again and again, God showed mercy and sent truth. Finally, because they refused to fear God and depart from evil, they were judged. Pay careful attention to what God told them. There is a line drawn in your life; I do not know where it is, but God will not allow you to cross it. He will reach the point where He says, "I'm not going to put up with those dirty clothes any longer. You better come and get those clothes clean. I am not going to allow that dross to just sit there on the surface." If you continue to refuse to repent, you will reach the point where God says, "That's it."

I am 56 years of age. This year, 2009, is the first time in my adult life that I am worried about our culture, our country, our churches, and our Christianity. We are seeing things take place so rapidly. We are seeing a decline so rapidly away from God. We are literally amusing ourselves to death. If you look up the definition of amused you will find that 'a' means 'without' and 'mused' means 'thinking.' Amused literally means 'without thinking.' Just pop in another video, take another trip, or drink another latte, and close your eyes to the truth; but I tell you God's judgment is on its way. It is not because of Washington; it is because of iniquity in the hearts of the people of God. Remember that the ultimate reason Sodom was destroyed was that Lot failed to reach his own family. Specifically speaking, today in Christianity, I am talking about Bible-believing Christianity, we are only a few years behind the world when it comes to iniquity. The things that were intolerable and unthinkable fifty or even twenty-five years ago are being found in the church today! You say, "Oh, I don't think God's judgment can happen in America." The most prosperous country in the world in 1930s was Germany. They recovered from the Depression faster than any other nation. They had the greatest scientists; they had a great level of prosperity; their future looked very bright indeed. In just six years, one unknown and obscure man rose to the top and led that nation of intelligent and accomplished people to mass murder and eventually to ruin. Do not think that it cannot happen to America. If there has ever been a time for us to think soberly and live righteously, it is in this generation. God has bestowed upon our country incredible mercy, and he has invested an enormous amount of truth in our country. If we refuse to fear Him and turn from our sin, we have no right to expect anything other than what God did for the apple of His eye, the children of Israel. They reached the point where He said, "No more purging; now the fire of judgment" and America will too unless God's people respond to mercy and truth with purging iniquity and fearing Him.

chapter 13

The Best Grape Juice I Ever Tasted

*Mercy and truth preserve the king; and his throne is upholden by mercy.
—Proverbs 20:28*

*I have not hid thy righteousness within my heart; I have declared thy
faithfulness and thy salvation: I have not concealed thy lovingkindness
and thy truth from the great congregation. Withhold not thou thy
tender mercies from me, O Lord: let thy lovingkindness and thy truth
continually preserve me.—Psalm 40:10&11*

*Thou wilt prolong the king's life and his years as many generations.
He shall abide before God for ever: O prepare mercy and truth, which
may preserve him.—Psalm 61:6&7*

M ercy and truth are vital for every child of God, but they are especially vital for those in a leadership position. Whether it is a pastor or a parent, a deacon or a teacher, a shift supervisor or manager at a plant, anyone who is leading others has a special need for these two balancing traits in their life. What the Scriptures tell us specifically is that mercy and truth have a preserving power. When something is preserved, it maintains its original characteristics. When someone is preserved, in this case a king or a leader, then he maintains his position of leadership and authority.

When I think of something being preserved, my mind goes back to my childhood. The best grape juice I ever tasted was made by my mother. In the late summer and early fall in southwestern Michigan, we would harvest the deep, purple, sweet, plump grapes. Mr. and Mrs. Smith were members of our church then, and they had a vineyard in their backyard. Mother and other ladies of the church would make jellies and jams and preserves and grape juice out of those grapes harvested from Mr. and Mrs. Smith's vineyard. We had a machine that squeezed the juice out of the grapes, and then Mother would boil the juice with sugar and pectin. Then, she poured it into squeaky clean canning jars and put on lids and rings and then sealed them in a pressure cooker. When they were done, she would set them out on the counter to cool down. I had a little metal basket which held maybe seven jars, and it had a little handle on it. I would carry them downstairs to the cellar where my father had built massive shelves because mother did a lot of canning.

Because of the canning process, the grape juice would stay sweet and fresh for years without spoiling or fermenting. I remember hot summer nights when we would get one of those jars out of the cellar, put a little ice in it and drink the best grape juice I have ever had. Just as the sugar and heat that sealed the jars preserved the grape juice, God says there is a way to preserve your leadership and influence over people. Leadership is not a constant thing. It is very delicate. Without mercy and truth, you will not have followers for long, and a person without a follower may be called any title he likes, but he is not a leader. In my analogy to grape juice, mercy is like the sugar, and truth is like the heat. Without both, the grape juice would spoil, and without both mercy and truth, your influence will wither away.

Solomon had the privilege of growing up in a home with a father who was a great leader. David is a wonderful example to any business person, pastor, parent—anyone who is a leader. Most people are oblivious to the extent of their influence. No matter who you are, there are people looking to you as an example. Influence is not something to be trifled with. When it is lost, the consequences reach far beyond your own life. They can touch the lives of thousands of people over many generations. So, it is important that we understand how to preserve our leadership. David was a man of great mercy and great truth. He had the necessary balance. By the way, that is not something that just magically happened when David became king. If you go back and read the story of his life before he took the throne in the latter part of First Samuel, you will see David demonstrating both mercy and truth toward others. Solomon could look back and see the pattern for his own rule and leadership in the life of his father.

Of course, saying that David was committed to mercy and truth does not mean that he was perfect. But, when he sinned and was rebuked, he repented. He did not allow the distance and the time that he was away from the Lord to extend to decades in his life. He got right with God, and his heart turned back to God. Even in his last days as an old man, David was still committed to mercy and truth rather than becoming self-centered and just wasting away the last years of his life, feeding his own desires and his own wishes and wants. We find David generously and studiously preparing for the marvelous temple that Solomon would build for God's glory. He poured his resources into it. What a wonderful testimony!

When David died, Solomon began his reign following the example of his father and ruled with mercy and truth. When we looked at the life of Bathsheba, we saw the upheaval that Solomon had to endure before he ascended the throne. He could have taken over and started seeking revenge against those who had opposed him. He had the power, but he showed mercy and offered those men a second chance instead of having them killed. Solomon followed the example of his father. The most famous story of Solomon's wisdom is when he was able to determine which woman was the real mother of the living child by threatening to cut the child in two and give half to each woman. The people were impressed with his understanding and commitment to truth.

The blessing of God was on his life and his leadership, and Solomon's fame spread across the world. In First Kings 10, we read of his meeting with the Queen of Sheba. This story gives us a great insight into Solomon's reign and the balance he maintained. To appreciate her reaction, you need to understand who the Queen of Sheba was. She was not from some poverty-stricken land. She had power and possessions in her own right. She came from a nation of great wealth and opulence; and yet, she was astonished when she saw the kingdom that God had bestowed to Solomon. She saw the amazing balance in his life and his maturity.

And Solomon told her all her questions: there was not anything hid from the king, which he told her not. And when the queen of Sheba had seen all Solomon's wisdom, and the house that he had built, and the meat of his table, and the sitting of his servants, and the attendance of his ministers, and their apparel, and his cupbearers, and his ascent by which he went up unto the house of the Lord; there was no more spirit in her. 1 Kings 10:3-5

If we were saying it today, we would say Solomon took her breath away. If someone came in to evaluate your leadership and influence would they be blown away and left breathless? God preserved Solomon's throne. God preserved his authority and leadership. Here is how the Queen of Sheba summed up what she had seen in Solomon's court. *"And she said to the king, It was a true report that I heard in mine own land of thy acts and of thy wisdom. Howbeit I believed not the words, until I came, and mine eyes had seen it: and, behold, the half was not told me; thy wisdom and prosperity exceedeth the fame which I heard. Happy are thy men, happy are these thy servants, which stand continually before thee, and that hear thy wisdom. Blessed be the Lord thy God, which delighted in thee, to set thee on the throne of Israel: because the Lord loved Israel for ever, therefore made he thee king, to do judgment and justice." 1 Kings 10:6-9*

Wow, what an incredible statement to be made concerning

Solomon's leadership capabilities! I think you would agree with me that Solomon's kingdom was being preserved, and that he was following the example of David in balancing mercy and truth. But sadly, that is not the whole story. Earlier, we looked at how Rehoboam allowed mercy and truth to run away from him. We focused on his foolish response to the people before, but now I want to draw your attention to the complaint the people made about Solomon's rule.

And Rehoboam went to Shechem: for all Israel were come to Shechem to make him king. And it came to pass, when Jeroboam the son of Nebat, who was yet in Egypt, heard of it, (for he was fled from the presence of king Solomon, and Jeroboam dwelt in Egypt ;) That they sent and called him. And Jeroboam and all the congregation of Israel came, and spake unto Rehoboam saying, Thy father made our yoke grievous: now therefore make thou the grievous service of thy father, and his heavy yoke which he put upon us, lighter, and we will serve thee. I Kings 12:1-4

Wait a minute. The Queen of Sheba said it was a blessing to be in Solomon's kingdom. Was she wrong? No. The problem was that Solomon changed. What happened to Solomon? He started out following his father's example of ruling with mercy and truth, but he did not continue with them. In fact, when Solomon died, the children of Israel said to his son, "Your dad was a tyrant and a taskmaster." Solomon lost his mercy. He lost his care for people; and in so doing, he created exorbitant taxes that stripped them of their wealth and took away their incentive to work. "Why should we labor when it is all going to be taken away from us?" At the end of his life, his country was seething with bitterness, hostility, and anger towards their king. You can begin with mercy and truth, but if you are not careful, you can lose your influence and position of leadership.

When did Solomon lose his leadership standing with his people? Where did he go off track? I believe Solomon lost his mercy after he chose to forsake his truth. First Kings 11:1 draws back the curtain for us. It says, *"But king Solomon loved many strange women together with the daughter of Pharaoh."* He started well, but Solomon in his middle years, blatantly disregarded God's commandment in Deuteronomy 17 concerning kings and leadership. God commanded the kings of Israel not to marry foreigners. The wives of Solomon turned his heart away from following God. Once Solomon lost the truth, mercy fled away as well. It is just like those jars of delicious grape juice. Once the seal is broken, the juice will only stay fresh for a little while. When we allow ourselves the pleasure of sin; when we crack open the lid just a little bit, it will not be long before we lose the sweetness of our mercy too.

After Solomon had become a self-centered, egotistical, arrogant old man, he died and left the kingdom to his son Rehoboam. Rehoboam, unlike his grandfather and his father, did not even at the beginning of his reign concern himself with having any mercy or having any kind of transparent honesty with the people. In fact, look again at how he responded when the people came to their new king and said, "Listen, will you please lighten up? Show us a little mercy here."

And he said unto them, Depart yet for three days, then come again to me. And the people departed. And king Rehoboam consulted with the old men, that stood before Solomon his father while he yet lived, and said, How do ye advise that I may answer this people? And they spake unto him, saying, If thou wilt be a servant unto this people this day, and wilt serve them, and answer them, and speak good words to them, then they will be thy servants for ever. But he forsook the counsel of the old men, which they had given him, and consulted with the young men that were grown up with him, and which stood before him: And he said unto them, What counsel give ye that we may answer this people, who have spoken to me, saying, Make the yoke which thy father did put upon us lighter? And the young men that were grown up with him spake unto him, saying, Thus shalt thou speak unto this people that spake unto thee, saying, Thy father made our yoke heavy, but make thou it lighter unto us; thus shalt thou say unto them, My little finger shall be thicker than my father's loins. And now whereas my father did lade you with a heavy yoke: my father hath chastised you with whips, but I will chastise you with scorpions.
1 Kings 11:5-11

There was absolutely no mercy in Rehoboam's answer. Look at the progression. Israel went from David who balanced mercy and truth from his youth, to his dying days to Solomon who balanced mercy and truth as he started, but later compromised with his flesh; and as a result, lost both to Rehoboam who did not have or want either mercy or truth. He started out as a self-centered, arrogant, and egotistical king and saw his nation divided by a horrible civil war. Now, I want you think about those three generations and ask yourself this question: where are you now and where are you going in relation to mercy and truth? Are you setting a godly example that will positively influence those you lead and those who will come after you? Are you faithfully praying that God will make you and keep you filled with mercy and truth? Your sphere of influence depends on mercy and truth. That is the only combination that will preserve your leadership.

The man that I admired more than any other man other than my father was my pastor during my teenage years. He was a man of incredible compassion. In 1966, he founded the church I grew up in. We started out in a little house; then with just a handful of families, we rented a schoolhouse. We began meeting there Sunday morning, Sunday night, and Wednesday night. We saw the church grow. My pastor was a wonderful, wonderful man of humility. What a gifted preacher! What a soul winner! What a man of compassion! But, when the seal on his jar broke, it all came tumbling down. The fracture of the trust that he had gained, the loss of the leadership and influence that he had with people, and the fallout of a decision to abandon mercy was painful. We can start out with mercy and truth; but if we compromise with sin, we are going to lose our truth, our transparent honesty. We will also lose our mercy and we will forfeit our leadership along with it. What a needless tragedy. Guard your heart. Guard your life. Do not let mercy and truth run away.

chapter 14

Joseph: Unstoppable Though Hurting

But the Lord was with Joseph, and shewed him mercy, and gave him favour in the sight of the keeper of the prison. And the keeper of the prison committed to Joseph's hand all the prisoners that were in the prison; and whatsoever they did there, he was the doer of it. The keeper of the prison looked not to any thing that was under his hand; because the Lord was with him, and that which he did, the lord made to prosper. Genesis 39:21-23

There is a reason that more of Genesis is devoted to the life of Joseph than to any other character. He is a shining example of Christian living, and an incredible Old Testament picture of the coming life and ministry of Jesus Christ.

His combination of mercy and truth certainly provided him with favor and good understanding in the sight of God and man. That does not mean everything went smoothly for Joseph; he suffered through a great deal of pain and heartbreak. In fact, if you carefully study the story of Joseph in Genesis, the most often mentioned thing that Joseph did was to weep! But, through everything that happened, Joseph received the favor of God. Everywhere he went, from Potiphar's house to the prison to Pharaoh's palace, Joseph prospered and succeeded in what he was given to do.

So, let's study the life of Joseph more closely to see this process in action. There is no question that Joseph was a man of consistent mercy and truth. The focus on Joseph begins when he was just a teenager, and we see him doing right regardless of what anyone else did. Genesis 37:1–3 says, *"And Jacob dwelt in the land wherein his father was a stranger, in the land of Canaan. These are the generations of Jacob. Joseph, at seventeen years old, was feeding the flock with his brethren; and the lad was with the sons of Bilhah, and with the sons of Zilpah, his father's wives; and Joseph brought unto his father their evil report."* Joseph faced a choice. He would have been a lot more popular if he had sacrificed truth, but he would have lost the blessing of God. Joseph refused to cover for his brothers. He took his responsibilities seriously and was faithful to fulfill everything he was asked to do by his father.

Joseph had a rocky relationship with his brothers because of the favoritism showed to him by his father Jacob. Joseph was the child of Rachel, Jacob's favorite wife. Though he had a younger brother who might normally have been his father's pet, Rachel died giving birth to Benjamin, so Jacob transferred his affections to Joseph. This had a devastating impact on the entire family. Joseph's brothers hated him because of the favoritism he received. Genesis 37: 3 & 4 says, *"Now Israel loved Joseph more than all his children, because he was the son of his old age: and he made him a coat of many colours. And when his brethren saw that their father loved him more than all his brethren, they hated him, and could not speak peaceably unto him.*" Verse 5 says, "*…they hated him yet the more.*" Verse 8 says, "*…And they hated him yet the more for his dreams, and for his words.*" Verse 11 says, *"And his brethren envied him."* This was a family with a lot of problems. But while Joseph was not perfect and did make some mistakes, he remained committed to mercy and truth.

Joseph's brothers hated him so much that when the chance arose, they sold them into slavery. They went home and told their father that Joseph had been killed by a wild animal. Twenty years passed before Joseph met his brothers again. Now, their roles were reversed. Where once he had been helpless and pleading for mercy he did not receive; now he had the power to mete out the vengeance they deserved. But instead, Joseph showed them mercy. He had so many chances to let mercy and truth escape; he refused to allow that to happen.

Sometimes, we do what is right, and it does not immediately result in positive blessings, but that is where our faith in God comes in. We quit so rapidly.

I was counseling with a man some time ago who was far, far away from God; and as a result, he was struggling in his marriage. He called me and said, "I'd like to talk with you." I sat down and talked him about his dilemma, and I gave him some advice and counseled him about a specific area. He actually started taking the advice and putting it into action. Then, he dropped away, and I did not see him for a while. I contacted him and said, "Hey, I've missed you. What's going on?" He said, "Well, you know I tried that Bible business, and it didn't work." I said, "You only tried for it six months." He said, "Yeah, but even after six months, she still divorced me." That's our problem—we want to put God on our timetable. If you approach the subject of mercy and truth with the attitude of, "I'm going to try this, and if it doesn't work, I'm going to move on to something else," then I can guarantee that you are going to be moving on to something else. God is not a Genie in a lamp that you rub like Aladdin and He comes out and says, "I will grant you three wishes." God does not work that way.

But, while God does not always work on our timetable, He does always have a plan. Everything that happens to us is according to His purpose. We see this clearly stated in Psalm 105:17 which says, *"He sent a man before them, even Joseph, who was sold for a servant."* Stop and think about the events of Joseph's life. He was hated by his brothers, they put him in a pit, they sold him to the Ishmaelites; he was bought by Potiphar, he was falsely accused by Potiphar's wife, then he ended up in prison, and he was forgotten by one of Pharaoh's servants for two full years. Now, look at those all of those events. How would you then describe what took place? God describes them as "Him sending a man." I do not know about you, but if God is going to send me somewhere, I prefer a different way to get there!

I would much rather God come to me and say, "I'm going to send an air-conditioned chariot to move you over to Egypt. I want to get you strategically placed the Egypt. There is a famine coming, and you are going to help the Pharaoh there. I have a beautiful condo on the sea there for you and an endless bank account. You can go there and just enjoy yourself, and it will be a wonderful thing." Now, that is how I would like for God to move me from one place to another. But, God did not do that with Joseph. God sent him through numerous injustices to get him to the place where He would use him to rescue the nation of Israel, though still small in number, and ultimately to preserve the line of the Lord Jesus Christ. God accomplished His purpose through adversity.

Joseph was successful because he was a young man who, despite all that happened, was still committed to trusting God enough to say, "I'm not going to give up. I'm going to keep dispensing mercy and truth, even though I'm in a prison." God gave Joseph favor and good understanding with that prison keeper and later on with Pharaoh. Joseph was unstoppable. Notice that the Lord was with Joseph. Verse 21 plainly declares it. Now, I know there is a sense in which the Lord is everywhere. But, when the Bible says the Lord is with someone, he's talking about a special level of companionship and relationship. Joseph was far away from home and all the people he knew, but he was certainly not alone. Joseph could not see God with his eyes, but you do not need to see God to know that He is with you.

Because God was with Joseph, He made all that Joseph did to prosper. As a result, Joseph kept getting promoted. Every time he got knocked down, he got promoted to an even higher level than he had achieved before. Never expect your Christian life to just keep getting better and better and better with nothing ever going wrong. Your circumstances are going to change. They are not always going to be pleasant, but you can always remain resolute. We must always remain resolute in our determination to obey the Word of God, not allowing the injustices of others to destroy our commitment to mercy or truth. Joseph's relationship with the Lord, I believe, was the key to his ability to keep that vital commitment.

It is not hard to be a person of mercy and truth when you are prospering and everything is going well. But, what will you do if you are thrown into a pit, falsely accused, or thrown into prison? Will you trust God when you cannot see what He is doing in your life? Are you unstoppable? Will you continue to love and care for people even if they do not love and care for you? Are you resolute in your determination to live by the truth of God's Word in spite of living in a society and an even in current Christianity that seems to be careening far, far away from the old paths? Whether we are in days of ease or days of difficulty, we need to be like Joseph. We need to be resolutely determined to be balanced Christians, to be giving mercy and to be giving truth. The only way that can happen is if we have the Lord with us because it is not in our power to do it; only in Him and through His strength can we maintain this balance.

God is good to us and shows us mercy even in times of sorrow, in times of heartache and in times of difficulty. Your circumstances may not be ideal. They may even be very, very painful, but yet the Lord is good even in those times of stress. He is always good. He wants to show you His goodness. If you will look for it, you will discover God and His character and attributes even in prison-like circumstances. Because Joseph was unstoppable, he experienced amazing opportunities to serve. It just astounds me that Joseph gained favor with the keeper of the prison. Because of our Reformers Unanimous program, I have spent a lot more time in jails and prisons and with the legal system than ever expected! It has been my observation that prisoners usually do not think very highly of the inmates. They tend to view them with extreme suspicion and even disregard. However, this was not the case with Joseph. The keeper of the prison placed the entire operation into his hands! Joseph was literally running the prison. Look at Genesis 39:22&23 again. *"And the keeper of the prison committed to Joseph's hand all the prisoners that were in the prison; and whatsoever they did there, he was the doer of it. The keeper of the prison looked not to any thing that was under his hand; because the Lord was with him, and that which he did, the lord made to prosper."*

Even in prison, Joseph prospered. I am glad to know that we can prosper in a society that is turning rapidly away from God. You know that God is not limited from helping us prosper personally, even though as a nation we are seeing the hand (I believe) of judgment from God. We can still be blessed of the Lord. Joseph is a living example of the benefits and blessings that come if we will remain unstoppable in our commitment to be filled with mercy and filled with truth in spite of our circumstances. God has great blessings available for every one of us if we will remain unstoppable. Where are you in your relationship with God?

Perhaps right now you are enjoying His favor in times of plenty, but even if you are in the time of poverty and a time of pain, God is still with you. God still has blessings available for you, and God can still give you unusual service opportunities that you never dreamed possible, despite those circumstances. God is preparing you for ministry opportunity that you never dreamed possible. Often, it is at our greatest times of pain and suffering, that we are introduced to ministry opportunity.

Twenty-one years ago, God graced our home with Janelle, our handicapped daughter. Not long ago, I was thinking back to how God has changed my life for the better through that set of circumstances that I would not desire for anyone else, but I also would not trade with anyone else. Has there been difficulty? Of course difficulty came to our home. Have there been days when we have wished that this cup had passed from us? Certainly! Would I change things if I could? Not for a second. This is God's doing, and He has used our circumstances to give us incredible opportunities. Even if you are in a prison of circumstances right now (or even a real prison), that cannot stop you from being an unstoppable person of mercy and truth. No circumstances can stop you from loving people and showing them mercy. Only you can decide to stop yourself. Do not do it! Just be outrageous about giving mercy. Sure, they do not deserve it; give it to them anyway. It will be good for you even if it does not have an immediate impact on them. Do not compromise the truth. Do not compromise your convictions. Remain determined to serve the Lord and to do His will. God will have special blessings and ministry opportunity for you; and more importantly, He will be with you. He will give you favor and good understanding, both with Himself and with those around you. Keep plowing ahead and keep growing strong. The results will amaze you!

chapter 15

Blend and Balance to Savor the Flavor of Favor

For yourselves, brethren, know our entrance in unto you, that it was not in vain: But even after that we had suffered before, and were shamefully entreated, as ye know, at Philippi, we were bold in our God to speak unto you the gospel of God with much contention. For our exhortation was not of deceit, nor of uncleanness, nor in guile: But as we were allowed of God to be put in trust with the gospel, even so we speak; not as pleasing men, but God, which trieth our hearts. For neither at any time used we flattering words, as ye know, nor a cloak of covetousness; God is witness; Nor of men sought we glory, neither of you, nor yet of others, when we might have been burdensome, as the apostles of Christ. But we were gentle among you, even as a nurse cherisheth her children: So being affectionately desirous of you, we were willing to have imparted unto you, not the gospel of God only, but also our own souls, because ye were dear unto us. For ye remember, brethren, our labour and travail: for laboring night and day, because we would not be chargeable unto any of you, we preached unto you the gospel of God. Ye are witnesses, and God also, how holily and justly and unblameably we behaved ourselves among you that believe: As ye know how we exhorted and comforted and charged every one of you, as a father doth his children, That ye would walk worthy of God, who hath called you into his kingdom and glory.—1 Thessalonians 2:1-12

There is incredible power in a partnership. When we blend personalities, when we blend spiritual gifts, when we blend mercy and truth, God can use that to accomplish incredible things for His Kingdom. The missionary team of Paul, Silas, Timothy, and Luke, a team of godly servants of the Lord, partnered together to bring the Gospel to the people at Thessalonica. In this description, the Apostle Paul gave of their ministry, you can unmistakably see the beautiful blend of both mercy and truth that can develop when partners in ministry build each other up and shore up each other's weaknesses. It was no accident that Jesus sent the disciples out two by two. That is because, in teams, they could blend, and they could balance each other. That meant that when they went someplace, they could meet the needs of people more effectively. Let's look at what this effective blended ministry looks like from the words of the Apostle Paul.

First, notice that this type of ministry is never in vain. Paul and his team went to Thessalonica, a place where the Gospel had never been preached before. Look at what happened in verse one, *"For yourselves, brethren, know our entrance in unto you, that it was not in vain."* As a team, they worked together in that community and brought blended balance into that community; and they presented the Gospel message of Jesus Christ. Blending and balancing as partners together is essential to our success in ministry. Notice also that they were not preaching their own opinions; they were declaring the whole counsel of God. The Word of God will effectually work in a person who accepts it in faith. (1 Thessalonians 2:13)

It is crucial that we focus on God's truth and not merely man's opinion. I know people sometimes come to church and go away saying, "I don't agree with that." That is just his opinion. If the message is from the Word of God, it is not just somebody's opinion; it is powerful, and it is truth. It is the perfect, eternal, and unchanging Word of God. It should not be a surprise if the absolute truth of the Gospel is not readily received. When Jesus preached in the synagogue in His hometown of Nazareth after His baptism by John, the people heard words of grace and truth, but they did not accept them. In fact, Luke 4:28&29 says, *"And all they in the synagogue, when they heard these things, were filled with wrath, And rose up, and thrust him out of the city, and led him unto the brow of the hill whereon their city was built, that they might cast him down headlong."* His own hometown people tried to kill Jesus when they heard Him preach!

Many people in ministry beat themselves up unnecessarily when the results of their labor are not immediately what they expect. They wonder, "What did I do wrong? I gave the truth. Maybe I was not merciful enough; or maybe I had too much mercy and not enough truth." Maybe you were out of balance, but if the perfectly balanced Jesus Christ Himself could be rejected, the problem may not be with you! Never forget that even if people do not accept the message, your ministry is not in vain. Because God has allowed me to stay in one place for many years, I have been privileged to see the process work itself out. Do not allow yourself to be discouraged if you don't see immediate results.

The second thing we notice about this team ministry was that they were bold in presenting the gospel. *"But even after that we had suffered before, and were shamefully entreated, as ye know, at Philippi, we were bold in our God to speak unto you the gospel of God with much contention."* If you do not have a blended, balanced ministry, when people begin rising up and being angry and upset, mercy will say, "You better quiet down, after all you're offending people." But, truth pulls the balance and says, "Hey you can't compromise. You've got to tell them the truth. They have to know that Jesus is the Savior and that He rose from the dead. Go on, speak up, and tell them the truth." When mercy and truth blend together, balancing each other, the result is a bold proclamation of the truth. Anything short of a bold proclamation of His Word will be grossly ineffective in ministering to people. When we present the truth of God's Word, it must be presented with great and honest confidence because it is not man's word. It is the living Word of God we boldly present to others.

However, we need to be aware that doing this right does not mean that people will love us and everything will just fall into place. Paul said they were "shamefully entreated" at Philippi. If you go back and read Acts 17, you will see that simply for casting a demon out of a woman and preaching the gospel, they were illegally beaten and thrown into jail. Paul got chased out of town, beaten up, arrested, and falsely accused nearly everywhere he went. When the Gospel goes forth and truth is presented, even when it is blended with mercy, it will very likely cause contention. Boldness is necessary to keep doing right in spite of what people do or what people say. In verse three, Paul talks about "exhortation." Exhortation is not lecturing people; it is literally calling them alongside with us. The same word is sometimes used for the ministry of the Holy Spirit in our lives.

When we present the truth boldly, we will dull its effectiveness if we do not speak to people with the truth from a position of drawing them alongside, of encouragement and exhortation. It is important that we hate sin but still love sinners.

Let's take a look at Paul's method of exhortation. First, he says, "It was not of deceit." The word deceit means "with a purpose to lead astray." There are some people who are very bold and blunt in what they say but their motives are wrong. The sword of the Spirit is sharp, but its message will be dulled if it is delivered from a hypocritical heart. Second, Paul says there was no "uncleanness." This word uncleanness literally means "a heart that is dirty." As we saw earlier, we are commanded to be vessels that have been purged and made clean to be fit to use. Finally, Paul said they had no "guile." The word guile is a fishing term which means "to catch with bait." What is your purpose? Are you working from ulterior motives, or is your purpose building God's Kingdom and bringing Him glory?

Notice the motive that was behind the work Paul and his team did. Verse four says, *"But as we were allowed of God to be put in trust with the gospel, even so we speak; not as pleasing men, but God, which trieth our hearts."* They were conscious of their responsibility and accountable unto God. They recognized what it meant to be "put in trust"—to be counted on to take care of something for another—with the gospel message. They were not driven by a desire to please or be accepted by men; but rather, their goal was to be pleasing to God. And, as Paul noted in verse five, they never forgot that God was watching everything that they did. *"For neither at any time used we flattering words, as ye know, nor a cloak of covetousness; God is witness."* Mercy and truth when properly blended and balanced, looks at our own hearts before looking at the needs of others. Yes, we need to be absolutely bold in our presentation of the truth, but we also need to do a thorough check of our own motives, a thorough check of our own hearts, and make certain that we are living our lives in such a way that we can say we are unselfish in our presentation of the truth.

One of the complaints I hear most often from Christian people who are away from God is hypocrisy on the part of believers. Sometimes, that is just an excuse for them; but unfortunately, the reality of how we personally live does not always match up with how we proclaim the truth. You will undo all your efforts in trying to help someone by proclaiming the truth to them if, in the course of that process, your own dirty heart is manifested. If they find out that you have dirt in your life, you will have nearly ruined your opportunity to proclaim the truth to them in a meaningful, effective way. Having been ministering for a long time does not protect you from falling. Paul and his team were very, very effective because when they did proclaim the truth, they were bold in their presentation, and they were also pure in their heart. Some people who have great boldness and know the truth wonder why they are ineffective in trying to help people and motivating them to turn their hearts and lives to the Lord. If that describes you, maybe you need to take a long hard look inside. Our ministry effectiveness is greatly hindered if we are not thoroughly right with God.

Then, Paul described a balanced ministry as being gentle in its demeanor. Verse seven says, *"But we were gentle among you, even as a nurse cherisheth her children."* Paul boldly proclaimed the truth, but he did not sacrifice a proper demeanor. You would not find that apostle becoming angry and mean spirited or vulgar in his conversations. You can speak the truth, but if you do it in a harsh or demeaning way, it ceases to be effective. Paul illustrates gentleness by talking about a nurse taking care of a little baby or a dear friend willing to give anything to another.

Paul also describes his ministry as that of one whose behavior is being carefully observed. In verse 10, he said, *"Ye are witnesses, and God also, how holily and justly and unblameably we behaved ourselves among you that believe."* People are watching you all the time. They are not simply listening to what you say; they are watching how you live. Nothing undercuts the effectiveness of our message faster than people observing that we do not behave ourselves in a biblical way. This is equally true whether we are teaching and training believers or trying to reach unsaved people with the gospel message. If you listen to the same jokes that everybody else listens to at the shop or your place of business; if you watch the same things; if there is no difference between you and the world, you might as well just be quiet. No matter how boldly you talk, your life is going to speak much more loudly.

Paul likens his balanced ministry to a father with his children in verse 11. *"As ye know how we exhorted and comforted and charged every one of you, as a father doth his children."* I know that not everyone has the privilege of growing up with a godly father who expressed his love and guided his children. But, there is nothing sweeter than a close parent-child relationship. My 12-year-old son, Justin, still comes in to say good night to me. I would not trade anything for the time we spend together, talking about the things of God, praying for each other and for God's work in our church and our lives. I have never seen a parent shout and berate a child into good behavior. But, I have seen patience and love work amazing transformations. You are not going to shout anybody into getting right with God. You are not going to criticize anybody into getting right with God. You are not going to insult anyone into getting right with God.

Finally, Paul said his ministry was successful because it was eternal in its vision. Verse 12 says, *"That ye would walk worthy of God, who hath called you into his kingdom and glory."* This is the vision that Paul and others had when they first came to Thessalonica. Why do people do ministry? Sadly, some people do it for personal, selfish reasons. Paul said, "I want you to know that our vision for you is that you walk worthy of the vocation in which God has called to you; worthy of His kingdom; worthy of

His glory." Oftentimes, our efforts to help people with the truth of this Word are curtailed and hindered because we lose sight of the eternal nature of our purpose. Paul and his team started out focused on the long-term goal, and they kept that focus no matter what else was going on around them.

After all is said and done, it really is not about our comfort. It is not really about changing people to benefit us or even ultimately to benefit them. It is ultimately for Him.

The church in Thessalonica was not just great while Paul and Silas and others were there, because those people were not focused on pleasing Paul and others. They were not just toeing the line because someone, a spiritual leader, a mentor was overseeing them. They caught a vision that they could walk worthy of the vocation that God has called them fulfill. That is absolutely essential, but it will never happen unless we continually work in this matter of blending and balancing our mercy and truth in presenting God's Word to others. Your ministry, whether to an entire church or a single individual, will succeed to the extent that it matches this pattern established by Paul and his team.

chapter 16

How God Addresses Our Imbalance

But it displeased Jonah exceedingly, and he was very angry. And he prayed unto the LORD, and said, I pray thee, O LORD, was not this my saying, when I was yet in my country? Therefore I fled before unto Tarshish: for I knew that thou art a gracious God, and merciful, slow to anger, and of great kindness, and repentest thee of the evil. Therefore now, O Lord, take, I beseech thee, my life from me; for it is better for me to die than to live. Then said the LORD, Doest thou well to be angry? –Jonah 4:1-4

We have talked a lot about the importance of balance. A few years ago, our family got a very vivid illustration of this truth. Dianne and I were on a cruise celebrating our anniversary. While we were out at sea, our cell phones did not have any reception. As soon as we pulled into port in Juneau, Alaska, both of our phones started going crazy. We had urgent messages. I immediately called the church, and they told us that our son Jason was in the hospital in critical condition. While he was riding his motorcycle, he had lost his balance and hit a tree. We nearly lost our son because of a lack of balance. And, a lack of balance between mercy and truth will destroy our effectiveness for the Lord in the same way. We see this principle illustrated vividly in the life of Jonah.

God called Jonah to go to preach His message of repentance to Nineveh. It was such a huge city that there were 120,000 children who were so young that they did not know their left hand from their right. Nineveh was a humongous, wicked city, a city of gross violence and the capital of the Assyrian Empire—the bitter enemies of the nation of Israel. However, God loved those people too, just as He loves all sinners. But, Jonah refused to go. You know the story. He went to Tarshish, got on a ship, found himself in a storm, and ended up being swallowed by a great fish. After that, he changed his mind and went to Nineveh and preached as God had commanded. The whole city, from the king down to the animals, was fasting and clothed in sackcloth and ashes. Everyone in the city was frightened into submission unto God, and they repented. Jonah 3:10 says, "And *God saw their works, that they turned from their evil way; and God repented of the evil, that he had said that he would do unto them; and he did it not.*"

Now you would think that any preacher would be happy with a revival like that, but Jonah was not. Why? Jonah was unhappy because he was real light on mercy and pretty heavy on truth. He was not interested in those people being converted. He wanted to see them destroyed. He had deep seated prejudice against them. In Jonah 4:1, it says that Jonah was displeased "exceedingly." The word means "the nostrils swelling and opening up." Jonah refused to go to Nineveh, not because he was afraid of what they would do to him, but because he was afraid they would listen to him, and God would spare them. In effect, Jonah was saying, "God, frankly Your mercy makes me angry." Jonah was heavy on truth, but light on mercy. He was out of balance; and as a result, he refused to help undeserving people. God said, "Go to Nineveh." He said, "No." Jonah was completely unconcerned about the eternal well-being of the people of Nineveh. Normally, we wouldn't say, "I want someone to go to hell", but Jonah really wanted them to go to hell.

I also want you to see that because Jonah was out of balance, he resisted corrective measures. He got on board the ship going to Tarshish, and God sent a storm. Why was the storm sent? It was sent to wake Jonah up. It was sent to make Jonah change his mind. But, Jonah resisted God's corrective measures. In fact, Jonah was down below the decks snoring away during the storm. It is amazing to me that Christians can be so oblivious to God's actions. He speaks to us, and we don't even recognize it at all. Even the unsaved mariners recognized the hand of some deity at work. They said, "This is no normal storm." These seasoned sailors were in fear for their lives. They woke Jonah up and asked him what was going on. God will use people and problems as corrective measures to try to bring us back into balance. When I say Jonah resisted God's corrective measures, it is not an exaggeration to say that at all. He even spent three days and nights in the belly of the fish before he cried out to God. I don't think I would have lasted that long! But, when we get out of balance between mercy and truth, we are going to behave just like Jonah. We are going to be unconcerned and uncooperative.

To top it off, Jonah was uncompassionate. He reported for duty, but his heart was not in it. I think he was laughing and rubbing his hands with glee as he shouted out, "Yet forty days and Nineveh shall be overthrown." This was a message of judgment delivered without any compassion. Jonah did not show them any plan for changing the situation. He did not even tell them to repent! Why? Jonah did not want them to change. The King actually did a better job preaching than Jonah. He said, "Listen, maybe God will change his mind if we repent of our evil and our violence and put on sackcloth and ashes. In fact, I command everybody in the city to do this. In fact, I do not want you to even feed your animals. When you put on your sackcloth, I want you to pour ashes on your animals too. We are going to cry out to God because we are serious about this matter. We do not want to die." When Jonah got out of balance, he was unconcerned, he was uncooperative, and he was certainly uncompassionate. He resented the Ninevites for receiving mercy from God.

God pressured Jonah to help people that he did not like because He wanted Jonah to add mercy to his truth. God punished him for his disobedience. If you tell God no and do not have any storms, you are probably not one of God's children. Obedience is not a game. God peeved Jonah by saving the people of Nineveh. He was still trying to get Jonah's attention to bring him back into balance. Finally, God prodded him with personal discomfort. Remember this—nothing happens to a child of God without a purpose. The decision is up to us. We can continue to rebel and resist and refuse to do what God wants us to do, but He is going to keep working to try to bring us into balance.

Let's look at the other side from the life of Peter in the story found in Galatians chapter 2. Here is someone who became heavy in mercy and light in truth.

And when Peter was come to Antioch, I (Paul) withstood him to the face, because he was to be blamed. For before that certain came from James, he did eat with the Gentiles: but when they were come, he withdrew and separated himself, fearing them which were of the circumcision. And the other Jews assembled likewise with him, in so much that Barnabas was also carried away with their dissimilation. But when I saw that they walked not uprightly according to the truth of the gospel, I said unto Peter before them all, If thou, being a Jew, livest after the manner of Gentiles, and not as do the Jews, why compellest thou the Gentiles to live as do the Jews? Galatians 2:11-14

Because Peter was out of balance, his decisions were made out of fear, rather than faith. Why did Peter change his behavior when the Jews from Jerusalem showed up? He did it not because it was the right thing to do, but because it was the convenient thing to do. He said, "I'm afraid of what people will think about me." Peter needed a big dose of truth; a renewed commitment to doing right. His fear wrecked his testimony. Peter's conduct had a major negative effect on the church. There was a division, a church split, which was so severe that even a good man like Barnabas was caught up in it, all because Peter lacked truth in his life. When you compromise the truth, it will not only hurt you, it will hurt a lot of people as well.

Notice the word "dissimilation" in verse three. It means "gross hypocrisy." In other words, Peter was living hypocritically. As a result, his walk became corrupted; and even worse, the gospel message became clouded. Peter's catering to the prejudice of the Jews from Jerusalem confused the Gentile believers regarding whether salvation really was of grace or partly of works. Being out of balance is serious business. Do we understand that? We tend to try to excuse it. We say things like, "Oh well, I've got so much mercy I don't want to hurt anybody's feelings. I don't want to ruffle anybody's feathers." We must commit to do what truth says whether people like it or do not like it. If it is the right thing to do, ultimately God will honor it, and God will bless us for it. We did not get into this for a popularity contest.

Because Peter was out of balance and because God loved Peter, He said, "He needs a big dose of truth. I have a pretty strong voice for truth." In fact, wherever he goes, they say, "Man that guy skins us alive wherever he preaches; that old fellow Paul. He is flat mean." (Nobody ever doubted Paul's commitment to the truth!) So, God sent Peter to Antioch; and when he showed up, he ran head on into the voice of truth. Paul got right in his face and said, "Peter, you are wrong." Whoa! Do you know what a lesser man would have done? What a lot of Christians do. "Well, I'm just going to find a nicer church. I want people to make me feel good. I don't go to church to feel bad." Imagine what would happen if you did that when you go to the doctor. When we get out of balance, we need the voice of truth. God has a way of sending someone who may irritate the fire out of you, but God has them there because He is committed to you becoming balanced in your life.

Because Peter was out of balance, Paul confronted him and he confronted him personally. He did not send down a magazine or a letter to every other preacher in Galatia, Macedonia, and Jerusalem to say, "I want to tell you what Peter's doing. He's a compromising preacher." Paul had the courtesy to go eyeball to eyeball with Peter and tell him his fault. He did it publicly before the entire church. Why did he do that? First, I believe it was because Peter was the public figure, and those in leadership have a greater accountability. It is one of the great problems we have in Christianity, even fundamental Christianity today. A man in spiritual leadership will mess up morally, and will quietly just be moved away until things settle down. Pretty soon, he's pastoring somebody else's church, and the new church does not have a clue because the issue was never dealt with publicly as it should have been. No wonder people do not have the fear of God when spiritual leaders can do such things and nobody ever holds them accountable.

There's a second reason why this rebuke was public, and that is because this was an opportunity for Peter to exercise humility and receive grace from God, which he did. Peter could have said, "Who do you think you are? I'm one of the original twelve Apostles. Get out of my face Paul. This is none of your business." Peter did not have that attitude or spirit at all. He recognized the problem and repented that he was out of balance in his life when God sent him the voice of truth. God cared about him enough to send him somebody who would tell him the truth, so he would know what he ought to do. By the way, though Paul was direct and truthful, he was not mean or insulting to Peter. He did not call him names or attack his character; he just pointed out his error.

I told you before how I got right with God when I was about sixteen years of age. From that time on, I had a burden to witness to my public school friends. On Sunday night, I would take a packet of tracts from our church tract rack, and the next day, I would go to school with my New Testament in my pocket. Our little church was growing. We were meeting in the gymnasium for activities where we played volleyball and basketball. I worked at a dairy, and I came in straight from work. I had my tennis shoes on and was ready to go when I walked in the door. Somebody called out, "Hey, come and be on our team." So, I reached my back pocket, and I took out my New Testament and slid it across the gymnasium floor. I threw it on the ground like a hockey puck, and it was about a second after it hit the surface, when all of a sudden this booming preaching voice that sounded like the voice of God or Moses called my name, "Paul Kingsbury!" He wanted everybody, especially me, to know who he was talking to. It was silent as a church in that gym when the preacher spoke, and you could still hear my Bible sliding across the floor. "Come here!" He put his finger in my face right in front of all those people, and he said, "Son, don't you ever treat God's Word that way." "Yes sir," was the only thing I said. My preacher gave me a good old-fashioned dose of truth that day, and I needed it. God loves you too much to let you stay out of balance. Just make sure you listen to His voice and those He sends to put things right. You will be very glad you did.

chapter 17

Where to Obtain Mercy

Seeing then that we have a great high priest, that is passed into the heavens, Jesus the Son of God, let us hold fast our profession. For we have not an high priest which cannot be touched with the feeling of our infirmities; but was in all points tempted like as we are, yet without sin. Let us therefore come boldly unto the throne of grace, that we may obtain mercy, and find grace to help in time of need.
—Hebrews 4:14-16

Over and over in Scripture, we see people desperately crying out to God for mercy. Whether it was the sick, the crippled, or the demon-possessed, these people came to Jesus seeking His mercy for their problems. Since Jesus returned to Heaven, where can we go for mercy when we need it? Hebrews 4 tells us that when we have expended all of our mercy and need our supply replenished, we can find it at the throne of grace. Who is the "we" that finds mercy? It is the kind of person who is at that point in their lives when they say, "I need more compassion. I need to give compassion to someone who does not deserve compassion, they deserve consequences; but instead, I need to exercise mercy in their behalf. Oh God, I am a person in need of more mercy!"

What is it that brings a person to a position where they are conscious of their need for mercy from God? Let's begin in verse 1, *"Let us therefore fear, lest, a promise being left us of entering into his rest, any of you should seem to come short of it."* These people who are conscious of their need for God's mercy are motivated to come boldly to God for mercy because of fear. I understand that Jesus said, "Fear not" oftentimes to his disciples. There are some things we should not fear; but at the same time, there is a healthy fear that every Christian ought to have. That fear spoken of in Hebrews 4 refers back to God's working with the children of Israel. Moses led them out of bondage in Egypt toward the Promised Land. That was the destination that God prepared for them—a place where they could rest from the labors of hundreds of years of slavery. But, they did not get there. They never got to enjoy the rest God had prepared for them. Because they refused to enter the Promised Land after the bad report of the ten spies, they wandered and wandered and wandered, but they never got anywhere. Israel stayed in the wilderness until that entire generation except for Joshua and Caleb were dead.

Are you discontented with an empty, meaningless, pointless life where everything just focuses on you and your own pleasures? Have you found out that what you have is not satisfying; so you get another goal; and then, when you reach it, you find out it's not satisfying either? I want my life to count for Jesus Christ. I want to know that I made a positive difference in this world. I want my wife and our children to know that I was a man of God, and I had an influence in their life. I want to be a faithful pastor. However, I live with fear of falling short of that goal. I do not want to do anything, be anything, or go anywhere that will ruin the potential that I have for Jesus Christ in this life. So, I am motivated by that fear. People who are conscious of their need for God's mercy are motivated by fear.

Second, people who seek God's mercy are motivated by the Word of God. Hebrews 4:12 says, *"For the word of God is quick, and powerful, and sharper than any two-edged sword, piercing even to the dividing asunder of soul and spirit and of the joints and marrow, and is a discerner of the thoughts and intents of the heart."* The Bible is alive, and it beats with the heartbeat of Jesus Christ. It is far more than just pieces of paper in a bound book; it is the living Word of God. That means it is current for every generation. It was good for the Old Testament; it was good for the inter-Testament; it was good for the New Testament; and it is good for the no testament time without end in the future. It will always be the Lord's book. If the Bible is doing what it should in your life, it will be like a two-edged sword. Swords are very motivating. If I said, "Move out of the way," you might say, "Why should I?" But, if I had a sharp two-edged sword, and I poked you with it, you would move out of the way without any argument.

It is tragic, but many people have a relationship with the Bible that does not move them. As a result, they are not very conscious of their need for God and His mercy in their lives. When God's

Word starts piercing and dividing asunder your soul and spirit, you are going to be motivated to go to God for help. When it begins to cut you, when it begins to reveal, as He says here in this verse, "the thoughts and intents of the heart," you see your need for mercy very clearly. Think about your thought life. Aren't you glad there is not a little monitor where everyone can actually see and hear what you are thinking? When people are cut by the Word of God, it drives them to seek God's mercy.

Christians who see God's mercy are conscious of the presence of God. Hebrews 4:13 says, *"Neither is there any creature that is not manifest in his sight: but all things are naked and opened unto the eyes of him with whom we have to do."* There is no clothing that can cover your nakedness from the Lord. He sees you the way you really are. A Christian who is motivated and moved to come to God's throne and say, "God, I need mercy" is inevitably a believer who has been confronted by the omnipresence of God. Do we understand that God is everywhere personally? He is everywhere personally so much that he lives inside the believer. That is what makes us a holy Temple unto the Lord; God living inside of us. When we lose consciousness of that, that He's watching us (He knows us intimately), we lose sight of how much we need mercy. But, when I know He is looking at me and sees me just as I really am, it motivates me to go to His throne of grace and ask for His mercy because I know that what He sees is not always good.

Christians who seek God's mercy are conscious that they need mercy first before they can extend mercy to others. Hebrews 4:14 says, *"Seeing then that we have a great high priest, that is passed into the heavens, Jesus the Son of God.*" When we offer mercy to people who do not deserve it, there is a tendency for us to start feeling sorry for ourselves. There's a tendency to get disgusted with them and say, "You know what, I'm just tired of this. I've given you mercy and given you mercy, and I'm tired. I don't have any more to give." You cannot buy mercy at Woodman's or Wal-Mart or the grocery store. The only place to get it is from God. When you go to God because you need mercy to give to other people, it reminds you of the fact that you really need mercy for you. When you run out of mercy for others, it is because you have lost sight of your need for mercy from God.

Finally, the person who seeks God's mercy is conscious of the fact that without it they will lose their grip. Hebrews 4:14 says, *"let us hold fast our profession."* The idea behind this is that of our losing grip on the rope that is keeping us moored from drifting away. You can drift just imperceptibly. You do not notice it; it happens slowly. That is the analogy that is used here; that we can lose our grip on that which moors us. Your profession is the testimony of your Christian life. Our covenant we have made with God was when we confessed that we belong to Him. Now, we are conscious of the fact that we are losing our grip on that testimony. This motivates us to turn to the Lord Jesus and to seek His help.

How then may we obtain this mercy from God? Verse 15 says, *"For we have not an high priest which cannot be touched with the feeling of our infirmities; but was in all points tempted like as we are, yet without sin."* We want to start with considering the Lord Jesus Himself. I want you to remember in your need for mercy, that you have a Savior in Heaven Who understands your dilemma. Jesus never did drugs, but he knows what it is like to have a craving that is almost overwhelming, a desire to escape reality. He knows what it is like to be tempted to go get drunk. He knows what it is like to go into illicit sex. He knows what it is like. Every temptation that we will ever face in our lives, Jesus faced a similar temptation, yet without ever yielding to sin. How could God have mercy on a sinner except God take on the form of a sinner and endure what it is like to be a sinner? That is how Jesus can be our merciful and faithful high priest. When you have need of mercy, you need to consider Jesus and run to that throne of grace.

Second, to receive mercy we must come boldly. This phrase means "to approach frankly, bluntly, candidly, truthfully, and with confidence." I know we all have certain "canned" prayers. If I asked you to pray for a meal, and you pray for the meal, chances are next week if I ask you to pray for a meal, it is going to sound very much like the prayer you said last week. I am not being critical of those things at all, but when the Bible talks about coming boldly before the throne of grace, it means "to come with a transparent honesty." This is a person who comes to God and says, "Life has brought me to the very end of my rope, and I'm losing my grip. I have no more mercy to give them. I need mercy from You, or I am not going to make it."

I live on Riverside Boulevard, on the other side of Interstate 90 from our church. There is a bridge there that I think they have been rebuilding for a hundred years now. When you go eastbound on Riverside, there are signs up that say stay in right lane, lane closure ahead. When I get to McFarland Road, I have to get in the right-hand lane. I am following the traffic laws and I am in the right lane, even though there is more traffic there. Invariably, someone comes along in the left lane and tries to cut into my lane in front of me at the last second. What is the natural reaction? I want to give them a piece of my mind. I want to lay on the horn. I want to cut them off. What do I do? I flee to the throne of grace for more mercy! I do not want to give them any mercy at all, but I need to. That is the way my life is…and the way your life is. There are always going to be people around us who need mercy and then need more mercy.

What do you do when you run out? You stop and think about the wonderful Savior we have Who loves you in spite of who you are, or where you are and what you have done; and you go back to Him and you say, "I'm here, and I'll admit to You that I don't deserve anything from You but judgment, but I need a big dose of mercy today." Come boldly to the throne of grace because the outcome is already settled; you can obtain mercy. The word *obtain* means "to accept with amazement." It is amazing that we can give mercy to others, but it is even more amazing that God extends mercy to us in the first place.

Let me close with this analogy. We talked earlier about our tendency to loosen our grip and let things drift. We have been offered "grace to help in time of need." This help is like taking a rope and tying our vessel tight to the moorings to stop our tendency to drift away." When you come boldly before the throne of God's grace, you will obtain mercy, you will find grace to wrap ropes tightly around your grip to help you stay tied to the moorings. So, where do we go when we run out of mercy? Go to Him. Go to that throne of grace, obtain mercy, and find grace to help in time of need.

chapter 18

Mercy, Truth, and Revival

To the chief musician, A Psalm for the sons of Korah. Lord, thou hast been favourable unto thy land: thou hast brought back the captivity of Jacob. Thou hast forgiven the iniquity of thy people, thou hast covered all their sin. Selah. Thou hast taken away all thy wrath: thou hast turned thyself from the fierceness of thine anger. Turn us, O God of our salvation, and cause thine anger toward us to cease. Wilt thou be angry with us forever? Wilt thou draw out thine anger to all generations? Wilt thou not revive us again: that thy people may rejoice in thee? Shew us thy mercy, O Lord, and grant us thy salvation. I will hear what God the Lord will speak: for he will speak peace unto his people, and to his saints: but let them not turn again to folly. Surely his salvation is nigh them that fear him; that glory may dwell in our land. Mercy and truth are met together; righteousness and peace have kissed each other. Truth shall spring out of the earth; and righteousness shall look down from heaven. Yea, the Lord shall give that which is good; and our land shall yield her increase. Righteousness shall go before him; and shall set us in the way of his steps. —Psalm 85:1-13 harles Haddon Spurgeon called the 85th Psalm the prayer of a patriot for his afflicted country. He expressed his belief that David penned this national hymn when the land was oppressed by the Philistines. When we come to the 85th Psalm, we are reading a passionate prayer for revival. In fact, if you will notice, the first seven verses are a prayer that God has inspired and recorded and kept for us that we might gain a better understanding of how it is that revival comes to an individual and to a nation. You cannot lose your salvation, but you can lose the joy of your salvation. You can lose the thrill of what it means to belong to Christ and to live for him and love him. That is the reality of life…and that is when we need a revival.

David begins his prayer with a look back at history and a remembrance of how God has favored Israel with revival in times past. Notice verse one, *"Lord, thou hast been favourable unto thy land: thou hast brought back the captivity of Jacob."* The word revive means "to make alive again." It is bringing back life to that which is dead or dying. When the Psalmist looked back on the days of revival that had come before, he saw a time of blessing and prosperity and the favor of God. When the children of Israel were in captivity because of sin, God brought them to a renewed freedom. Is that not what God wants to do in our lives? Is that not something that we could say we need personally? We would like to return to the place where we are no longer bound to sin but where God has stepped in and brought us out of captivity, releasing us like prisoners being released from jail.

In verses two and three, we see how revival restores our

relationship with God. *"Thou hast forgiven the iniquity of thy people, thou hast covered all their sin. Selah. Thou hast taken away all thy wrath: thou hast turned thyself from the fierceness of thine anger."* I have no doubt at all that God is angry with us as a nation today. And, it is not "them" out there that is the problem; we are. I am talking about God's people. There is no question that we are in desperate need of an old fashioned Holy Ghost, God-sent revival. It is not the iniquity of the world that kindles God's wrath, but the iniquity tolerated, overlooked, and even enjoyed by His own people. When revival occurs, there will be remarkable forgiveness of sin and a turning away of God's wrath. Oh, how we need that today!

Look at the plea for revival David voices in verse 4, *"Turn us, O God of our salvation, and cause thine anger toward us to cease."* We do not hear much praying like this today. Most of our prayers are short and simple (and not very sweet). This is an earnest, fervent, passionate prayer from a man who means business with God. Prayers that do not bring tears to our eyes or a quivering to our lips or an emotion that torments the spirit do not produce revival. Why would God respond to passionless prayers? Until we are serious about our need for revival, it is unlikely that we will ever experience revival. When we reach the end of ourselves and recognize that is only through God that we can have life again, then we can expect revival. Let me ask you today, how important is revival in your prayer life? If we want the touch of God on our lives, if we want revival for ourselves and the people we care about, we are going to have to become serious about this matter of prayer.

What happens when a real revival comes? The answer is found

in verse six. *"Wilt thou not revive us again: that thy people may rejoice in thee?"* Revival always brings a renewed joy to our relationship with God. A person who experiences revival will rejoice in the Lord regardless of what else is going on in his life. You may be in times of great stress, difficulty, and challenge. There may be disappointments on every hand. But, when revival takes place, God's people rejoice, not necessarily in what is happening in their lives, but in what is happening in their relationship with God Himself. It is a rejoicing that is not born out of an appreciation for what God is doing for us, but of an appreciation for Who God is.

David concludes his prayer for revival in verse seven and then transitions to focus on what happens in the heart and life of a person who is looking for revival. Psalm 85:7&8 says, *"Show us thy mercy O Lord and grant us thy salvation. I will hear what God the Lord will speak: for he will speak peace unto his people, and to his saints: but let them not turn again to folly."* What signs can we look for to indicate revival is coming? The first thing David mentions is that God's people will be in tune with God's voice. God can speak to you, and when He does, you do not want to miss it. I have noticed in my own life, that when God is about to do something significant, His voice will become a priority to me.

The second sign of a coming revival is a renewed fear of the Lord. Verse nine says, *"Surely his salvation is nigh them that fear him; that glory may dwell in our land."* Do not let anyone deceive you about what it means to fear God; it is far more than just respect. The word fear here literally means "to tremble." When I was little boy, my dad was the primary disciplinarian in my home. Mom could get a switch off the neighbors willow tree and do a pretty good job with that, but what I really feared was my dad's belt. I mean that thing brought terror to my heart! There is a healthy fear that you and I need to have of the Lord. He is our perfect Heavenly Father, and He is simply not going to let us get away with sin. If revival is coming there will first be a return to a wholesome, healthy fear of the Lord.

Throughout this book, we have talked about the importance of mercy and truth. And in Psalm 85:10, we find that before revival comes, they must meet together. It says, *"Mercy and truth are met together; righteousness and peace have kissed each other."* The Hebrew word used here for meet together is very specific. It refers to two enemies or opposites coming together. David personifies mercy and truth and talks about them like enemies meeting at a negotiating table to conclude a war. It is not simply a meeting; it is a reconciliation, a commitment to future cooperation together. Mercy and truth tend to be opposites, yet before revival comes, they must be able to meet together and cooperate together.

What is true of individuals is true of churches as well. There are churches that tend to be strong in mercy and weak in truth. Unless they meet together with truth, they are going to be a compromising church, and they will eventually lose their testimony for God and will be ineffective. Fundamental Christianity is full of churches like this. They have fallen under the influence of those who counsel them not to ever be offensive or say anything that might hurt someone's feelings. You may gather a great crowd that way, but you will not build a great church. More importantly, you will not help people. They need the truth, whether they want to hear it or not.

Now, on the other hand, there are churches that are truth churches without mercy. Yes, they are fundamental and correct in their doctrine, but they have an attitude that absolutely cares nothing about sinners. I have been in some churches that say 'Fundamental Independent Baptist' on the sign with all capital letters, but they were as cold as an Eskimo's igloo. If you walk in there with any outward sign of worldliness, or look like you might be unsaved, you would get the stiff arm rapidly. There is no kind of welcome or friendliness there. If you ask them why they have that attitude, they would say, "Because we're committed to the truth here." That is not effective. You can hurt a lot of people with that commitment to the truth when there is no mercy.

So, what do we need? We need mercy and truth to meet together. I am 56 years of age, and I have been attending fundamental independent Baptist churches all my life. I have seen the entire gamut. I have seen the extremes, and neither one of them is pleasing to the Lord. Why do not we focus on the things that matter? Why do we not preach to help people find Christ and then to grow spiritually? You know, it is possible to preach against sin and still love sinners. I have watched people fall off the track on both sides. Some go to the truth; others go to mercy. But without both, you will fall.

One of the things that has been a major help to our church in this regard is Reformers Unanimous. Successfully working with addicted people absolutely demands a balance between mercy and truth. We have to reach out to these people and bring them to Christ, while at the same time giving them the absolute truth of God's Word. I think it has the potential to take churches that are strong in mercy and help bolster their truth and take churches that are strong in their truth and help bolster their mercy. The same thing is true of individuals. You are not stuck where you are. I believe all of us are more inclined to one trait or the other, but we can add the one we lack through the power of the Spirit of God!

Because mercy and truth are not meeting together, we are not seeing the power of God bring revival like we need to. Children who grow up in unbalanced homes are easy prey to the Devil. They will either yield to the flesh if there is no truth, or they become bitter because there is no mercy. New converts who grow up in the faith in unbalanced churches are easy prey to the Devil. Before revival comes, there will inevitably be a return of mercy and truth to one another.

I am simply calling you today to start seeking a genuine, old-fashioned return to sincere pleading and praying with God for revival. Ask God to send a revival to your life, to your home, to your church, and to our country. Let's get earnest and serious about this matter. Listen to God as He speaks to your heart. Bring mercy and truth together and let them cooperate, so that God might send a great old-fashioned revival to our land.